TONY GLEESON

◆

THE
LAST STEP

Complete and Unabridged

LINFORD
Leicester

First published in Great Britain

First Linford Edition
published 2019

A catalogue record for this book is available
from the British Library.

ISBN 978–1–4448–4299–9

Published by
F. A. Thorpe (Publishing)
Anstey, Leicestershire

Set by Words & Graphics Ltd.
Anstey, Leicestershire
Printed and bound in Great Britain by
T. J. International Ltd., Padstow, Cornwall

This book is printed on acid-free paper

DEDICATION:
To Sally and George, whose insight
kept me authentic

1

Closing time: it's pretty the much the same at drinking institutions everywhere. Faithful patrons have all heard the refrain: 'You don't have to go home, but you can't stay here. Drink up!'

And so it was that Toby found himself with his two new acquaintances standing outside the glass door to the Albatross, one of the last of the city's authentic regular-folks bars, watching the barman locking the door and switching off the neon light in the window. He absently glanced at his watch: 2:05 a.m. There was no need for any ceremonial farewells; the three of them simply wandered off lopsidedly in separate directions along the deserted halogen-lit street.

It had rained earlier in the evening and it was still damp and chilly. Toby zipped up his jacket and started walking briskly. He was surprised just how good it made him feel to realize he had hung out in a bar all night without starting a fight, not needing to prove himself. He could have civil words with strangers who weren't necessarily the enemy. Maybe he was finally growing up after all.

He knew he wasn't supposed to be drinking, but the bar had been the only quiet place he had found where he felt safe. A beer or two couldn't hurt. He didn't really feel all that drunk, though he did stumble a bit now and then. He had prided himself on nursing his beers all night. His wallet hadn't held all that much to begin with, but more importantly, he was taking this staying-out-of-trouble thing very seriously. His years at Wentworth hadn't been that terrible, all things considered, but he had no desire to go back. He had done a lot of stupid things as a kid and he hoped those eleven years had helped him grow up. That was one of the reasons he had deliberately avoided returning to his old neighborhood. His old crew was gone, but he didn't want to take the chance of running into anybody from his past, and besides, this hopefully impressed the parole officer about his good intentions.

His mind wandered, revisiting lots of the stupid things he'd done when younger, things that he didn't really want to start remembering again.

He'd stayed by himself in a booth in the Albatross, trying to formulate his new plan of action. Thinking came slow. He needed to find a job. Maybe a new trade. Stay out of trouble. Build a new life, little by little.

Most importantly: erase the past. He knew that was going to take time. He looked forward to the day when there would be that new life, maybe even a wife and a family, and those memories would no longer return to haunt him.

They weren't only stupid things he'd done, he realized. They were shameful, almost unbearably so. It occurred to him that he had become a person who couldn't stand the thought of who he had been before.

The only person from outside to ever visit him *inside* had brought a new idea: redemption. The concept had changed his head. Then that prison padre had started talking about it as well, and it had become something he wanted; possibly more than anything else. They made it seem a real, tangible thing.

Toby hoped it was.

Instinctively he reached into his pocket and fingered the beads the padre had given him. He still wasn't sure he bought the whole package the chaplain had been selling, but he thought about it a lot. Religion had never been his thing, and Toby had resisted what he called the padre's membership drives, but still, the priest had always been there to listen.

Only two people had ever given him the slightest flicker of hope. Now the flicker promised to grow in to something of a flame.

He hoped some of the plans he had come up with this evening would sound good to his parole officer tomorrow morning. By closing time, they had started sounding pretty good to him. It had all seemed a good omen, even the fact that the few patrons in the bar had smiled and said good night to him; the two tipsy guys and the matronly old lady who looked so concerned. He hadn't quite been ready to let down his guard around them, but something had told him that when he was ready, there would be people with whom he could actually get along.

Lost in his thoughts, he made his way to the complicated intersection of three large avenues at a roundabout. At this late hour, only a few cars moved around the circle. The quickest way to get home was via a stairway here that led down to the opening of the short tunnel where Pomeroy Avenue ran under the natural ridge of the traffic circle. It was a crazy, hilly part of town, two levels of streets and scattered staircases, endlessly confusing to visitors and new residents alike. There was still plenty about his new neighborhood he had to figure out, but Toby had quickly discovered the Albatross and the shortcut to get there from his boarding house and back.

The Pomeroy Stairs were an early discovery: thirty concrete steps from the circle down to a landing, a right angle, and twenty-nine more to its namesake avenue, just before the tunnel. Then it was a short walk, just a few blocks, to his street. The stairs themselves had low concrete handrails but were unlit. They were broad enough to walk safely down, and the ambient illumination from the streets kept them from being too dark. He wasn't particularly worried about muggers lying in wait; he knew how to take care of himself. Nobody had gotten the drop on him back in his old neighborhoods, and nobody had done so successfully at Wentworth before he had finally stepped away from confrontations. He stopped to catch his breath at the top of the stairs, looked down into the semi-darkness, and started the descent.

Four steps down, he began to hear the voice over the sound of the traffic. It was a woman's voice . . . urgent, worried. His eyes started to adjust to the dark and he saw her standing on the landing, looking down the stairs toward Pomeroy Avenue below, speaking rapidly into a cell phone.

He took a few more steps before she became aware of him and looked up directly at him. She was still talking into the phone. She wasn't speaking English.

He wasn't sure what the language was . . . not Spanish, of which he knew a fair amount. It sounded like it might be Chinese, or Korean, or something like that . . .

The woman, he now noted, was Asian, with long black hair spilling over the shoulders of her trench coat. It was difficult to tell how old she might be but she looked under thirty. When he reached the landing, she stopped talking and stared at him with alarm. He tried to smile reassuringly and raised his hands up in a gesture of pacification. He intended no trouble here.

'Don't be scared,' he said gently. He pointed across the landing to the second set of stairs. 'I'll just be heading down there.'

'Please help?' the woman said in halting English. She held the phone out to him. 'Need English. They not understand me. Please.' She held the phone out to him, her whole arm trembling. 'Please help?'

Toby sighed deeply. He reached out to take the phone from her. 'Sure, lady.' He put the phone to his ear. 'Hello?'

It was the last word he would ever utter.

★ ★ ★

Detective Jilly Garvey, stifling a yawn, reflected that she would have preferred a different way to start her day. The sun was just beginning to break through the early morning gloom. She and her partner, Detective Dan Lee, were squatting to either side of the medical examiner, who was gazing at a fourth, considerably less animated individual lying on the concrete.

'Your vic took two slugs in the chest at close range.' Mickey Kendrick, the ME, was using two gloved fingers to carefully raise one side of the jacket of the supine body sprawled across the landing. The blood had spread across the victim's sweatshirt before turning brown and caking. There was also a dried blood stain on the pavement beneath him. The murdered man was large and thickset, possibly in his early thirties, with a buzzed scalp and a thick beard that could not completely cover a scarred and pitted face. His head was rolled to one side, his eyes bulging in a lifeless stare. 'I'm not seeing any cartridges on the ground so my educated guess is a revolver. Preliminary estimate, time of death was around two last night. But this is the interesting thing.' He pulled back the jacket collar and pointed to the man's neck.

A small figure resembling a rimless three-spoked wheel had been carved into the side of his neck. It was little more than three insertions of a pen knife, radiating from a central hub at 120-degree angles to one another.

'He wasn't quite dead when this little pinwheel was done. It bled out a bit. Ever see something like that?'

Dan looked over at his partner. She pursed her lips and shook her head silently. Dan pulled out his phone and began to snap photos of the man's face and the odd mark.

Mickey dipped his head near the dead man's face and sniffed audibly. 'Our man was doing a bit of drinking last night,' he said in a monotone. 'Spilled it on his clothing too. He still smells like a brewery.'

Mickey's jowly bloodhound face and sardonic manner belied a sharp mind and a lot of experience. He was methodical, thorough, and, most importantly, expeditious with results. Both detectives appreciated that he was the examiner on the scene; his spare, mordant wit was just part of the package.

A couple of Scientific Investigation Division techs had begun to string a skein of yellow tape around the stairs and landing, and uniformed officers at both the top and the bottom were holding back the small group of curious onlookers that was gathering. Jilly decided she'd do a quick examination and then make room for the techs. She gingerly turned the body slightly to one side and checked the left-side pockets, sweeping her gaze across the murdered man.

'Still has his wristwatch and wallet, and there are other items in his pockets. This doesn't seem like a robbery.' With gloved hands, she eased out the flimsy wallet, which was sticking partially out of the back pocket of his jeans. It was little more than a slim folder of cloth and board.

'Not much in here. Twelve dollars. No driver's license but he does have a state issued ID, and a business card.' Jilly read the card. 'His parole officer. Maybe he's a recent release from the system.' She inspected the photo ID card, which looked brand new. The state Department of Motor Vehicles routinely issued these for non-drivers, and the portrait was one of their typical dreadful productions. 'Arthur Tobias. Age 31. The address is only a few blocks away.'

She eased the victim over and carefully probed into the pants pocket on the other side: a metal house key, a set of rosary beads, a pack of matches, and some small change. She read the name on the matches: 'The Albatross . . . Could be where he was last night.'

She held the plastic beads up for Dan, who was writing into his notebook while squatting. Dan nodded. 'Possibly some-one at a nearby church might have known him.'

'Kind of a long shot, but who knows;

we might end up grasping at straws on this one.'

Jilly fished a few transparent plastic evidence bags out of her pocket and carefully placed the matchbook, the beads, and the wallet's contents each within one. She stood up, sweeping a gaze across the landing and not finding anything to grab her attention. 'Anything you want to check out further?'

'I think I'm good. What's our next move?'

She looked up the stairs towards the already busy traffic circle, then down the other staircase towards Pomeroy Avenue. 'We're only a few blocks from the address given as his residence, down there, as well as the bar where he might have been last night, up that way. It'd probably be as easy to walk to them from here as to go get our car. I've even got sensible shoes on. How about it? I'm thinking the residence. Might be some kind of halfway house.'

Dan nodded. 'The bar's likely not worth checking out until later today, even if they did happen to be open now. If somebody there remembers him, they'd be on a later shift.'

'All right, then.' Jilly looked back at the dour ME. 'Thanks, Mickey. You and the techs can have Mr. Tobias.'

The ME nodded, never breaking his gloomy expression. 'I should be able to get him on the table tomorrow if I'm lucky. I'll let you know what I find. And be careful on those stairs.'

'What do you mean, Mick?'

'That last step is apparently a killer.'

Jilly and Dan turned to walk down the flight of steps to Pomeroy.

'It would stand to reason he was at a halfway house,' Dan said as they descended past the techs on the steps. 'And it seems he was doing some drinking. You'd think that would be a no-no at a rehabilitation home.'

'If it was a good one. We both know there are a few under the radar.'

★ ★ ★

The address was a large old Craftsman-style house tucked back off a side street

13

and shrouded in trees and bushes. A lanky bald man, probably on the other side of sixty, was in the front yard trimming the shrubbery as they came down the walkway, and he turned to unsmilingly greet them. They already had their badges and IDs out. He put down his clippers, yanked a large stub of a cigar out of his mouth, and said, 'What can I do for you?'

'Arthur Tobias,' said Jilly. 'This was given as his current address?'

'Oh yeah. Don't tell me the guy's gotten himself into trouble already. He's only been here a few days . . . '

'It might be better if we could go inside and talk,' said Dan. 'How about we do that?'

The owner of the house was named Arlo Merchant, and he boarded parolees on a contract basis with the state. He had the capability of boarding up to five individuals but at present he had only three. Each had their own room and shared the common areas of the house. Merchant seemed to find the need to defend himself and quickly volunteered that he was completely accredited by the state and in compliance with all regulations. As they sat around a rickety wooden table in the old but spacious kitchen, Jilly tried to sideline those issues and get back on track.

'What was the last time you saw Mr. Tobias?'

Merchant shrugged. 'Last night, I guess. What happened to him, anyway? Is he back in jail?'

'You guess? You don't have a bed check or anything like that?'

'Naw, not exactly. More like a head check in the evening. And a sign-in and sign-out sheet. But I go to sleep too, you know?'

Jilly and Dan shot a glance at each other. This guy wasn't just under the radar, he was off the scope.

'Mr. Merchant, Arthur Tobias is dead. He was murdered last night.'

'What? No way!'

Dan rested his chin on his hand and sighed deeply.

'He'd apparently spent some time at a local tavern and was heading in this direction sometime around two in the morning. Is that a common occurrence among your residents?'

'We screen for sincere individuals here, Detective . . . Gerber, was it?'

'Garvey.'

'Yeah, well . . . we discourage drinking, and no alcohol is allowed on the premises. And I look for signs of intoxication of any kind. Guy gets loaded, too many things can happen, and I guarantee he won't last here long. Next thing you know, back to the can.'

'So,' interjected Dan, 'we take it you are shocked, *shocked*, to discover one of your charges had snuck out to a bar all night.'

Jilly never ceased to be amazed at how quickly her normally staid partner was developing a sense of sarcasm. It seemed to fly over the head of Arlo Merchant.

'The guy struck me as pretty serious about getting back into society. And they're supposed to sign out if they leave the premises. Nobody signed the sheet last night. At least I don't think so.'

Merchant stood up, walked to a breakfront in the adjoining parlor, and picked up a clipboard. He brought it back to the kitchen, shaking his head.

'How about that. I guess he did sign out last night, around nine. Never signed back in.'

Trying not to roll her eyes, Jilly took the clipboard and looked at the sheet. Tobias was the only sign-out since late afternoon, and the only one not signed back in. 'Do you lock the door at a certain time, have any kind of curfew?'

'Not exactly. More like guidelines for when you should be here. I think it's important to leave 'em some responsibility. The door's locked at night, but of course they got keys.'

'So what do you know about Tobias before he got here? Where was he in prison and for how long?'

'He came from Wentworth State. Wait, I got papers.' Merchant rose from his chair and left the kitchen, returning shortly with a manila folder. He sat back down and opened it. 'Yeah, Wentworth. He did an eleven-year stint there.' He turned it so they could read it as well.

'That's quite a stretch. What was he in for?'

'Manslaughter and armed robbery is what it says. That's all I know.'

'Isn't it difficult for a con with a record of violent crimes to get accepted into a halfway house?'

'Depends on the guy's record in prison. Tobias had an excellent record at Wentworth and a good recommendation from the parole official there. It's on the sheet here, see?'

Dan perused the paper. 'You never talked to him, interviewed him before he moved in?'

'Oh sure. He didn't want to talk details. They never do. Mostly I told him the rules of the house, gave him his chores, stuff like that.'

'So you don't really know anything about him. Is that normal procedure?'

'Like I said, he was only here a couple, three days.'

'How about the other residents? Did they get to know him?'

'I'm not sure. Since he just got here, I'm not sure if he'd got to know the other guys yet.'

'Can they both be accounted for last

night? Both were here?'

'Nobody else signed out last night. Far as I know, they were both here.'

Dan sighed again. 'But then, you thought that of Mr. Tobias as well, didn't you?'

Merchant shrugged, looking uncomfortably abashed. The table got very quiet.

'So,' said Jilly finally, 'the other two residents . . .'

He stared back and forth at them dumbly for a long minute before the light dawned in his eyes. 'Oh, I guess you'd like to talk to them, huh?'

'If they're here, yes.'

'Les is probably getting ready to go to work, but Sammy ought to be here. Hang on.'

'We'd appreciate it if you didn't say anything about Mr. Tobias to them.'

Merchant nodded, left the room, and plodded up a set of stairs while Dan and Jilly exchanged looks, expressions, and eye rolls. He returned shortly with two apprehensive-looking souls who sat themselves at the kitchen table, blinking at Dan and Jilly. Merchant stepped back and leaned silently on the kitchen counter, arms folded.

'Did Mr. Merchant tell you why we're here?' Jilly began. They both shook their heads warily. Clearly he *had* told them they were detectives.

'We wanted to ask you both about Arthur Tobias, your housemate. Do either of you know him at all?'

Sammy, the heavy-set darker one, shook his head one more time. 'He's the guy who just got here the other day. Only said 'hi' to him a few times.'

They both turned to look at Les, the skinny guy with the long dirty blond hair. He shrugged. 'Same here. We had a short conversation the day he got here. Real short. That was about it.'

'And what was that about?' asked Dan.

'Just, you know, introductions. I told him he looked familiar. He said I didn't.'

'He tell you anything about himself?'

'Said something about just getting out. You don't really talk about yourself much with people you haven't gotten to know . . . '

'Doesn't strike me as a big talker,' Sammy added. The table grew very quiet. These were also pretty close-mouthed guys, Jilly mused, but that would make sense. There was also clearly a curiosity growing in both of them. She could sense the wheels turning in their heads. Had their new housemate gotten himself in some kind of trouble, and more importantly, how would that affect them?

'Did Mr. Merchant tell you that Mr. Tobias is dead?'

Their eyes widened at that and, out of sync, they each said, 'No!' and shot a glance at each other and back to the detectives. There seemed honest surprise in both of them.

Dan pulled out his phone and brought up the photos of Tobias. 'Is this him?' Both peered at the screen solemnly and nodded. Sammy uttered a quiet 'Damn!' under his breath.

'Would this mark mean anything to either of you?' He swiped to the photo of the odd slices on Tobias's throat.

They both shook their heads. Clearly getting a comment out of either was going to be a tooth-pulling exercise. Both detectives duly noted, however, that neither man had registered any kind of reaction to the mark.

'What about you, Mr. Merchant? Have you ever seen a mark like this before?'

Merchant walked over and stared at the screen of the phone for several seconds. 'No, I've never seen something like that. What is it, a propeller? A pinwheel? What's it mean?'

'That's something we're trying to figure out,' Dan replied, closing the phone's photo album.

Les cleared his throat tentatively. 'Could you guys excuse me? I'm gonna be late for work and that's not something I need right now.'

'Where do you work?' asked Jilly.

'I'm a mechanic at the Lube'n' Oil over on San Mateo. I've had the job since I got out, about two months now, and I'd like to keep it.'

'Sure,' replied Jilly, turning to Sammy. 'And what about you?'

'I work for a landscaper. Today's a day off.' He looked as eager as his housemate to take their leave. She obtained full names from both the men and told them they could go. It was like a teacher dismissing a class eager to head to recess. Within moments, only the two detectives and the caretaker remained in the kitchen. Merchant, staring dumbly, did not look any happier to be with them.

'Anything else you can add to help us out here?' Jilly asked finally.

'Me? No. No, not that I can think of. Man, this is terrible. This is gonna hurt my business really bad. I need that money from the state coming in.'

After a few more fruitless questions, they thanked him and left their cards, telling him to contact them if he had anything to add. Neither of them had much hope of that happening.

Returning to their car, they walked in thoughtful silence for almost a block before Dan finally spoke.

'Something seems to bother you about this one.'

Jilly nodded. 'This could be someone settling a score with Tobias. The guy's only a couple of days out of prison when someone walks up to him and shoots him at point-blank range. Then, before leaving the scene, the shooter takes the time to cut those odd marks in his neck.'

'Prison grudge?'

'That would make the most sense. He'd been in Wentworth for quite a while.'

'He was a big guy,' Dan added. 'Mean-looking, been in a lot of fights. I'm sure he could defend himself. He must have developed some wariness in prison, but he let someone get right up close to him late at night on a deserted stairway. So . . . it was someone that he knew, that maybe he trusted?'

Jilly nodded. 'Not only that, but a fairly cool customer. They were deliberate. They knew what they were going to do and took the time to cut that message into him.'

'Somebody with a grievance. They knew who he was and where he was. Could the killer have accompanied him from the bar?'

'Or followed him.'

'Is it possible,' asked Dan, 'that

someone ran into him by surprise at the bar, and decided to kill him?'

'Maybe. I don't think there was a confrontation or a fight. There were no signs of a struggle. He was stalked. Tobias was taken by surprise.'

'Witnesses who could help put this together are unlikely at that time of night. So why would the killer leave those marks as a message? A message for whom? Maybe there are more people involved in this.'

'Or,' Jilly said grimly, 'there are *going* to be more people involved. That's what worries me.'

As they walked, they rapidly worked out a plan of action upon their return to the unit. The first order of business would be to search all available records for Arthur Tobias and to talk with his parole officer. It also made sense to check the records of Merchant's other two tenants, Samuel Figueroa and Lester Lonergan. Jilly wasn't ready to dismiss delving into Merchant's own history a bit as well.

'Something else I'm interested in,' Dan said. 'Who found the victim and called it in?'

'We'll have to check that out. All we know was that it was a 911 call.'

'Whoever it was, I'd be interested in talking with them. I'll take that one.'

'And that bar, the Albatross.'

'Yeah, we should head over there this afternoon. Maybe we should split up the tasks. It's going to be a pretty busy day.'

He heard his partner heave a deep sigh. 'You really do seem to have a bad feeling about this one.'

'You got that right, Dan. Why do I think something's going to take a weird bounce on this one?'

'Uh oh. One of those premonitions again. Your gut worries me since it usually knows.'

'Yeah, well . . . here's hoping I get proven wrong.'

2

The Personal Crimes Unit was the usual hive of activity: people in motion, the constant undercurrent of voices, computers and telephones. Jilly remembered that when she had first arrived in the squad room as a detective, it had been known simply as Robbery-Homicide. For a short period of time the name of the unit had been changed to Special Crimes, before the Department had decided to bestow upon it the solemn title Personal Crimes, simultaneously changing the name of the unit one flight above them to Property Crimes. Throughout the cosmetic changes, the nature of the felonies her unit addressed had remained the same: murders, severe assaults, serious robberies. It was a territory that was never free and clear; the city obligingly dropped new crimes upon them in a constant barrage. All the detectives of the unit seemed to be playing an endless game of catch-up. Jilly and Dan didn't bother to greet any of their harried colleagues and simply dropped themselves down at their desk computers.

Jilly was able to glean a fair amount of information on Arthur Lee Tobias, age thirty-one. He was born and spent his childhood in the neighboring city of Sycamore. He had a juvenile record of a few minor offenses. In many cases, in their state, one's juvenile record would be erased after a few years if there were no subsequent serious offenses and the individual stayed out of further trouble. Unfortunately, that was not the case with Tobias. Only shortly after attaining his majority, Tobias had hit the big time, turning up in Midland City, a few hundred miles to the southeast, as a participant in an assault, robbery and killing, for which he was apprehended and sentenced to Wentworth State Prison. He seemed to learn a lesson in the process; his prison record was exemplary, and he was granted parole at his first hearing, after eleven years.

Jilly was able to glean a few details about Tobias's crime from the record. He and two other men had forced their way into a check-cashing establishment at closing time, beaten two security guards and a clerk, and taken the contents of the office safe. One of the guards had been assaulted so savagely that he had later died. On top of this, the three had escaped in a stolen car and hit two pedestrians as they sped away. They left a trail, it would seem, that could have been followed by a blind man; a police raid netted all of them by the next morning.

Tobias had apparently lucked out. He was the youngest member of the crew, just barely a legal adult, and couldn't be proven to be either the driver of the vehicle nor the person who had actually performed the assaults. He still received a fairly harsh sentence and, had he not toed the line while incarcerated, might well still be spending more years behind bars.

No present next of kin, and no family whatsoever, was listed. If Tobias had living relatives, they were no longer a part of his life.

Dan, meanwhile, had summoned up records for Figueroa and Lonergan and had feverishly jotted down notes on a yellow legal pad at his desk before moving on to explore the 911 call. A few phone calls and emails later, he had a copy of the voice record on his computer desktop.

'Jilly, you might want to come listen to this,' he called to her over the ambient noise of the squad room. She rose from her own desk and walked over to look over his shoulder.

'The call came in at 5:47 this morning. Anonymous caller, didn't want to leave a name. Called from a cell phone.'

'So no chance of tracing it beyond the provider tower.'

'Correct. Here it is.' Dan clicked his mouse. The audio came through the computer speaker.

'911, what is your emergency?'

'There's a dead guy here?' It seemed to be a young male voice, high-pitched, agitated, almost breaking into squeaks at moments, with that widespread and irritating constant upward inflection after every phrase. 'I'm at the stairs, near the tunnel on Pomeroy? I saw him up there, on the stairs! At first I thought he was just

30

a homeless guy sleeping — but then I saw the blood!'

'All right, sir, you say you're at the Pomeroy Stairs, near the tunnel?'

'Yeah, yeah, I guess that's right.'

'And you say there's somebody there who appears to be dead?'

'He *is* dead? There's blood? His eyes are wide open! Somebody killed him!'

'And what is your name, sir?'

'Look, I don't want to get involved. I just wanted to tell you about the dead guy? Goodbye!'

The call was ended.

Dan looked over his shoulder at Jilly. 'Quarter to six in the morning. Couldn't have been too many people around, at least not on foot.'

Jilly nodded. 'Maybe there are security cameras operating in the area.'

'Slim chance, but maybe. They're everywhere now.'

'It'd be worth talking to this caller, *if* we could find him. That's the problem with a cell phone. No way to trace the source of the call past the tower.'

Dan tapped some keys and clicked the

mouse a few more times and brought up a map of that part of the city on his monitor. He zoomed in to the immediate area, then gazed intently at it for a long time.

'He said the body was 'up there.' He was coming up the stairs from Pomeroy when he saw Tobias. He was heading for the traffic circle.' He hovered a finger over the map. 'He came from down here somewhere. Where could he have been going?'

'He sounded young. Maybe a student? The university's not far.'

'Maybe. Going to early class, you're thinking? Or an early morning job before school?'

'Good possibility. Here's what I got on Tobias.' Jilly summarized what she had just learned about the victim. 'Anything interesting on Figueroa or Lonergan?'

'Figueroa spent three years on a drug rap way out in Contreras, a medium security prison. He seems pretty minor league. No connection to Tobias that I could see. Lonergan, well . . . maybe it doesn't mean anything, but . . . '

'What?'

'Lonergan did six years downstate, at

Presa Vista state prison. About a year ago, he was transferred . . . to Wentworth. That's where he was when he was paroled.'

'So he and Tobias might have known one another there. He certainly didn't let on to that if it's true.'

'Interesting though that he *did* say that he thought Tobias looked familiar . . . ' Dan nodded. 'Seems another conversation with Mr. Lonergan is in order.'

They figured that this case would interest their lieutenant, Hank Castillo, so they decided to check in with him and fill him in on their morning. As usual, 'the Lou' was knee-deep in paperwork but his neatly organized desk and his own dapper appearance belied his constantly beleaguered status as head of the unit. His uniform — neatly trimmed salt and pepper hair and mustache, crisp white shirt, and three-piece suit, the jacket of which was draped over his chair — gave him an air of confident dignity even in the most harried moments. He waved them in and actually listened intently to their recap, nodding occasionally.

'If this is some kind of payback, like

you suspect,' Castillo said after they had finished, 'and there's a message behind it, maybe this killer isn't finished. I hope you're planning to mention this at the lunch sit-down today.'

Castillo encouraged his detectives to share ongoing case information on a semi-regular basis and tried to provide the opportunity to do so. Every few weeks, he would make a meeting space available at lunchtime for anybody who was free to confer. Most of the detectives agreed in principle it was a good idea in case someone else's case dovetailed in some details with their own; all of them had had the experience of missing a morsel of information that someone else had turned out to possess. But it was always a question of schedules allowing. It was routine to be overworked and behind time, or just off duty. Jilly and Dan exchanged looks. They hated to lose their momentum, but they had to admit he made sense. Jilly looked at her watch and nodded.

'We'll be there,' she said. Castillo nodded brusquely.

'Good, then. Keep me informed.' Without further ceremony, he lowered his head and picked up a document on his desk. End of audience.

'So what have we got,' Dan asked as they threaded their way around desks back to their own, 'about an hour or so, before we join this confab?'

'Yeah. Time to work out the afternoon's plan of action and then grab some lunch to eat at the meeting.'

'I'm guessing it's not going to take very long. For all we know, we'll be the only ones there.'

The meeting was held in one of the interview rooms, a spacious but hardly comfortable ambience: metal chairs around a metal table surrounded by walls with fading paint. Three other detectives from the unit had actually shown up, including Frank Vandegraf and his new partner, Athena Pardo, the youngest and latest addition to Personal Crimes. The third detective present was a genuine surprise: Marlon Morrison, who would charitably be thought of as somewhat unmotivated. Marlon was a long-timer, biding his time before he could retire on his pension by generally doing as little as possible. Frank and Athena looked up from paging through notebooks and nodded in greeting to them. Marlon simply looked bored as he fiddled with his phone and munched on a long sandwich.

'Looks like the gang's all here,' Morrison drawled. 'Pretty good showing today. Shall we get this over with?'

Dan and Jilly took seats. Before anyone could say a word, the door re-opened and two more detectives entered: Leon Simpkins and Art Dowdy. The partners made a strikingly disparate pair. Simpkins was tall, African-American, and outgoing; Dowdy was short, ash-blond, and taciturn. Some on the unit jokingly referred to them as the Emcee and the Mortician. Jilly recalled that Frank, ever the old schooler, had called them Mutt and Jeff a couple of times, referring to an old comic strip duo that probably meant nothing to half the unit. Jilly respected them as smart and focused. Simpkins especially, despite his ready smile and wit, was a serious investigator.

The proceedings, as usual, were informal and free-wheeling. Frank jumped right in with a quick rundown on the cases that he and Athena had caught in the past two weeks. Jilly got the definite impression that Athena had provided the organized precis; Frank was a methodical investigator but 'incisive' was not the word that came to mind about him as a rule. Maybe she was going to prove a good complement to her veteran partner.

Some back-and-forth exchanges around the table followed, a few remarks and jokes and an equally brief overview by Dowdy with added observations by Simpkins. Morrison made a few acid comments that related more to the burden of his job than to any specific case but managed to outline the bare bones of his current assignments. Jilly decided he had ducked into the meeting simply because it afforded a safe place to finish his lunch in relative peace. Finally Dan glanced at his notebook and briefly described two of their other recent case acquisitions, finishing with what they knew of the Tobias case. Simpkins seemed to find that one of interest. He stopped clicking his ballpoint pen and watched Dan intently, starting to take notes on a legal pad.

The three-line mark that had been

inscribed on Tobias' throat seemed to interest him particularly. He even asked Dan to draw it on his pad.

Jilly leaned into the table. 'Is this something that's familiar to you, Leon? Because if it is, we could definitely use some insight on it.'

Simpkins stared at his pad thoughtfully for a long moment, his brow knitted and lips clenched. 'I can't say for sure yet. It's definitely ringing a bell. I'll need some time to think about it and I'll get back to you.' He shook his head and then seemed to return his attention to the table.

The meeting quickly wound down and everyone rose without ceremony. Everybody still had a lot to get done and the day was slipping away.

'I'm thinking the parole officer is next,' Jilly said as they walked back to their desks. 'Edith Lincoln. I'll give her a call and see if she can see us.'

'Let's split up. I called the Albatross earlier and was told the owner was on last night. He'll be there shortly.'

'Okay by me. And we'll need to check out Wentworth.'

'That's about a two-hour drive each way. Hopefully some phone calls first can clear some hurdles. I can start making them this afternoon.'

★   ★   ★

'I began wondering when he missed his appointment this morning. I guess this is as good an excuse as I've heard.'

Edie Lincoln dropped a slim folder on her desk and plopped herself into her swivel chair. Jilly adjusted her original estimate of the woman's age: the facial lines and the white streaks in her dark hair now seemed to be premature, from stress. She leaned over the desk to stare expectantly at the detective sitting across from her. She had told Jilly she could give her ten minutes, and the clock was clearly running.

'What can you tell me about Tobias?'

Lincoln shrugged. 'We had an introductory meeting the day he got out, as is required by law. He told me where he was going to be staying, what kind of jobs he planned to be looking for; things like that.'

'So that would have been, what, Friday?'

Lincoln glanced at her desk calendar. 'Yes, three days ago. He struck me as serious about getting a new life in order, but you can't always tell. I get a lot of con jobs. I hoped he wasn't going to be one of them. I told him he could have the weekend to get himself together, but I expected to hear a specific plan of action by today. I knew he couldn't do much in the way of looking for a job over the weekend, but I wanted to make sure he was serious about what he was doing. I was also planning on an unannounced visit to his halfway house, which is routine with new parolees.'

'You had a gut feeling about him?'

'Somewhat. You get that after a few years at this. He struck me as . . . hopeful.'

'What made you see him differently? Was there something specific that you could put your finger on?'

Lincoln thought for a long moment before answering. 'There are a lot of people who come through here who are trying desperately to impress upon me just how earnest they are, how reformed, how sincere. They do a sales job. Tobias wasn't like that. He was strangely relaxed. He acted more like he was resigned.'

'Resigned?'

'At one point he said something to the effect that he didn't want to go back where he come from. He said . . . what was it? 'I can't be that person anymore.' It was like he had had enough. He seemed full of guilt . . . almost haunted. He wasn't interested in selling me. It was more like he needed to sell *himself* . . . that he was, like, redeemable.'

'Redeemable?' Jilly repeated.

'Yeah. I know, that's strange. I see all kinds of performances in here, Detective. I had a feeling this guy was the real deal. When he didn't show up this morning, my first thought was that I'd been wrong, that he was just another con artist.'

'Did you try contacting him to see why he didn't show up?'

Lincoln sighed. 'Hadn't gotten to it. I've got a load of nearly seventy cases right now. Not like I have the time to

41

drop everything to immediately chase down every stray lamb.'

'What about his contact information? Did he have a cell phone, or just the number of the house?'

Lincoln opened the folder and looked over the top sheet. 'At this point, just the number for the group home.'

'What do you know about that group home?'

'Not much. I think I had a case that lived there maybe two years back.' She stared up wearily over her heavy glasses at Jilly. 'They all start to run together after a while.'

'So you don't know anything about Arlo Merchant, the guy who runs the home?'

'As I said, I was planning an in-person visit to check it out and make sure Tobias was actually living there. Merchant seems to have been checked out okay or they wouldn't still be sending guys there. The system is overloaded and we have to work with what we have. New releases get sent to all kinds of places, even to their families. I'm sure it's no shock to you that some are better than others.'

'Any idea if Tobias had any family in the area? Where did he come from before he got sent to Wentworth?'

Lincoln paged through the few sheets in the folder. 'Apparently not. He gave no next of kin or relatives of any kind. He just applied and got into Merchant's home and submitted that as his new address.' Lincoln looked up. 'I can photocopy his file for you, for what it's worth. And you might find out more from his parole agent at Wentworth. That's who works out all the logistics a few months before the inmate is released.'

She looked at her wristwatch with a telegraph worthy of a stage actor projecting to a huge theatre. 'I'm afraid I've got to get back to the asylum, Detective.' She pulled a business card out of a desk drawer and handed it to Jilly. It was the same kind of card that Tobias had had in his pocket. 'If you have any more questions, feel free to shoot me an email.'

★   ★   ★

43

Lannie O'Casey was a big jovial Irishman with freckles, receding carrot-red hairline, and thick glasses. In his two decades as proprietor of the Albatross, he had seldom found it necessary to be outright unfriendly to a patron, and he was happy to explain that to Dan.

'Let me put it this way, Detective Lee,' he said in a lilt with the slightest hint of his New York Irish roots. Dan really wasn't interested in having it put any other way and simply wanted to move on with his questions, but O'Casey was such an affable fellow, he decided to humor him at least for a while. 'Everybody thinks, watching those TV shows and reading those books, that policemen are constantly drawing their weapons and shooting people, and certainly that's sometimes the case, is it not?'

'Sometimes, yes,' Dan said slowly, wondering where this was heading.

'But not always, am I right? Aren't there many cops who've seldom found it necessary to even draw their gun? It's my understanding that in real life, most cops have never fired their weapon, much less taken a life.'

'I can't authoritatively say most, but I know a few officers who haven't.'

'Well, it's a similar situation with your bartenders, you see. Everybody thinks that taverns turn into buckets of blood with regularity and that tending a bar requires one to be a combination of a prize fighter, a hockey enforcer, and a mob muscle man. I won't say there haven't been times when I had to make my point more strenuously with a particularly obstreperous drunk. But in general, what I find serves me in much better stead is a genial smile, an understanding word, and a goodly dose of diplomacy.' He continued to beam at Dan across the bar, finally casting a look down behind the counter. 'Of course, I do keep a shillelagh or two back here just in case, and once a few years ago I did find it necessary to produce a pistol upon which I make a point to keep my permit current. But in general, being a barkeeper is a much more peaceable profession than the average person would think.'

'I'm happy to hear that, sir,' Dan said, a trifle uncomfortably. He pointed to the photo on the screen of his phone lying on the bar top. 'So do you remember seeing this man in here last night? You did say you were bartending last night?'

O'Casey adjusted his glasses and stared at the picture. 'Yes I was. Sunday nights are generally Alice's night, but she called in sick and well, when you're the owner, you're the last line of defense. There's nobody I can call to come in for me, I'm afraid, whether I'm running a hundred-degree temperature or nursing a broken leg or whatever. So I took her shift. But it was a quiet night, only a handful of patrons, mostly regulars. A couple guys playing darts, like that.'

'So,' urged Dan, 'this person?'

O'Casey nodded vigorously. 'Yeah, he was here. Big guy, kinda mean-looking, bent nose and all that, but he had a relaxed manner about him, quiet, not threatening, you know? He ordered a cheap draft beer and nursed it at one of those back tables there. Refilled a couple times but didn't spend a lot. Some places, they get upset when the customer is taking his time, you know? I'm not like that.'

'Was anybody with him or was it just him?'

'It was just him,' said a hoarse voice from one of the back tables. Dan turned to see a fifty-something woman smiling over her shoulder at them.

'That's Wanda,' O'Casey smiled. 'She's sort of our den mother here. Always interested in what's going on.'

'Well, forgive me for listening in, dear,' Wanda said sweetly. 'I just thought I might be able to help.'

'You were here last night?' Dan asked.

'Wanda's always here,' O'Casey said. 'Surprised she doesn't pick up her mail here.'

'Now, that's an exaggeration, Lannie. You're going to give this nice young man the wrong impression of me, like I'm some kind of barfly or something. I just come here to watch out for you all.'

'Indeed, Wanda. What would we do without you?'

Dan tried once again to get this mad train back on the rails. 'Ma'am, did you talk with this person?'

'Only briefly. He looked quite troubled. I went over to ask him if everything was all right.'

'And he told you to mind your own business,' O'Casey interjected, 'did he not?'

'He was much nicer about it than a certain bartender I know would have been,' she sniffed. 'He thanked me for my concern but said he just had to do some thinking and work out some problems. He said he was putting together a plan to get his life back together. He sounded . . . very *dedicated*. So I left him alone.'

'And he stayed here until closing time?'

'He did,' said O'Casey. 'I announced last call about ten minutes to two. He brought his glass up to the bar shortly thereafter and said thank you and good night.'

'A nice young man,' Wanda said. 'Scary-looking on the outside, but sad on the inside.'

'Putting his life back together,' Dan repeated.

'Yes, that's what he said.'

'And then he didn't talk to anyone else here? And he left alone?'

'He did.'

'Was there anybody else left in the bar by then?'

O'Casey considered that. 'The two

guys who had been playing darts — well, by the end they were just sitting at the bar talking sports — and Wanda and myself. That's about it if memory serves.'

'That's right,' agreed Wanda.

'Do you happen to know either of them? Regulars?'

O'Casey shook his head. 'Nope, hadn't seen either of them before. Affable enough fellows. They were drinking dark beer, I remember.'

'Darts and dark beer. But they likely weren't Brits,' Wanda interjected with a bit of a slur and a ladylike hiccup. 'They were gentlemen of color, as I recall.'

'One does not preclude the other, Wanda,' O'Casey admonished. 'But Wanda's described them correctly. I detected no accents, at any rate. Seemed like locals, just unfamiliar ones.'

Dan pointed again to the phone screen. 'Did this person talk to the other two guys before he left?'

'Not really. I herded them out at closing right behind him. They all just exchanged brief pleasantries, the way happy inebriates tend to do upon leaving a place as nurturing as this, and headed off on their ways.'

'Did he walk away with either of the two?'

O'Casey thought about it. 'No. I'm pretty sure the other two went in the other direction from him. They both disappeared pretty quickly.'

'Is there any chance someone might have been waiting outside for him, or might have followed him from here?'

'Always the possibility, I suppose. But I saw nobody on the street while I was locking the doors. Just him, wandering off down the street.'

'You saw him walking away? Which way did he go?'

O'Casey pointed out the window. 'Down the street towards the circle. Otherwise, the street seemed empty.'

'And Lannie, being the gentleman he is, called my usual cab after locking up and made sure I got into it heading safely home,' Wanda added.

'So you haven't told me yet, Detective. Clearly something bad happened to this man?'

'I'm afraid so,' said Dan, pocketing his

phone. 'He died last night, not far from here.'

'Oh my good Lord!' exclaimed Wanda, crossing herself with such vigor that she nearly tipped over her wine glass. 'What happened?'

'He was shot to death on the Pomeroy stairs. I'm surprised neither of you heard about it.'

O'Casey shrugged. 'All the more reason we don't get a newspaper here and I seldom have the television on. People come to the Albatross to escape the harsh realities of that world out there. I'm saddened to hear the news. I hope he found the peace he was apparently looking for.'

Despite his earlier entreaties of the friendly character of the patrons of the Albatross, it was apparently not the first of his patrons that had met a tragic end. The barkeeper and his customer began an impassioned discussion of the short, brutish and unpredictable nature of life. Dan thanked them and quickly headed for the door, life on the other side of which perhaps was shorter and more brutish but, to his way of thinking, considerably less eccentric.

He turned towards the traffic circle and began walking, taking note of his surroundings as he did so. The most direct route back to the halfway house was down this street and across the roundabout to the Pomeroy stairs. It took him about eight and a half minutes to the stairway, allowing for getting across the crosswalk as traffic (most of it at any rate) yielded to the pedestrian as they were supposed to. It would have been easier to cross in the middle of the night.

The crime scene had been cleaned up and the tape removed; an unsuspecting pedestrian on the stairway would have no idea of the grisly event that had so recently occurred there. Dan stopped at the top of the staircase and gazed around and down. He saw no light fixtures on the stairs themselves. There was a street light near the top of the steps, but where the steps ended at the fateful landing and then continued to the right, down to Pomeroy Avenue, it would have been quite dark. The landing fell in a shadow between the illumination from above and below. Somebody could have been waiting for Tobias down there. Perhaps Tobias was a bit tipsy, in a hurry to get back to the house, lost in thought. Maybe his guard was down.

Dan swept his gaze around the traffic circle, looking for any possible security cameras that might have caught the scene. He walked down to Pomeroy and did the same thing. In modern-day urban America, it was against all odds to *not* find a security camera somewhere within a given radius. It was just a question of figuring out where it might be.

There was one possibility. As the traffic on Pomeroy Avenue entered the short Pomeroy tunnel, there was a flashing amber light with a sign that read in capitals CAUTION: SLOW FOR TUNNEL. Directly above the sign was one of the numerous traffic cameras that the city had installed a few years back in an attempt to deter, or apprehend, scofflaws who would speed up or otherwise ignore traffic signals. Legal challenges had largely curtailed the program, but a few of the cameras were still operational. If this one worked, its focus might have included the base of the stairs. Dan pulled out his notebook and jotted down the location. It was a long shot, and he hoped he'd find something with better promise, but he was determined to investigate every possible angle.

★   ★   ★

'Hey Art.'

Dowdy looked up from his computer to see Leon Simpkins, as if he had appeared out of thin air. He raised his eyebrows expectantly, pointed index fingers hovering over his keyboard.

'Do you think you can hold the fort down without me for a few hours tomorrow? I've got something that's come up and I just asked the Lou for a few hours of personal time.'

'Are you asking me,' Dowdy said dryly, 'or telling me?'

Simpkins broke out in a huge grin. This was the duo's typical routine. He clapped Dowdy on the shoulder.

'I knew you wouldn't mind. I'll try to get back by mid-afternoon.'

Dowdy ducked his head back down into his monitor and started hitting keys on his keyboard with two fingers. 'Hope the fishing's good,' he said, not looking up.

'I'll be close enough to say hi to the fish for you,' Simpkins replied. 'But the kind of fishing I'll be doing will be on dry land.'

3

Eddie Sutcliffe huddled inside his maroon hoodie, striding down Pomeroy Avenue apprehensively. It was still about fifteen minutes until sunrise, but there was already light breaking over the Tuesday morning traffic that was already building at this early hour. He hoped, as he neared those creepy stairs, that they'd be clear by now and back to normal. If there was still police tape or any reminder of what he had seen yesterday, there was no way he was going up there again. The longer 'back route,' circling around and up to the round-about as he had done yesterday, was a pain he hoped to avoid, but he had left earlier than usual in case that's what he had to do to get to the coffee house in time for his three-hour shift before classes started at the university.

It looked like he lucked out. The stairs were clear. He shuddered as he thought of what he had found up there yesterday morning, shook it off and began to jog up the steps, head down.

He was surprised to find a guy in a windbreaker sitting on the stairs, apparently reading a newspaper in the sparse light. A newspaper? If it wasn't one weird thing it was another. Maybe he needed to start avoiding these stairs totally. Eddie muttered 'Excuse me' to the man, who looked up and smiled, folding the paper as he slid over to make room to step past him.

'Looks like it's going to be a much nicer day than yesterday,' the man said pleasantly. 'The rain's passed, and it ought to be warmer.'

'Yeah,' said Eddie absent-mindedly. 'Nicer morning than yesterday.' He had taken a few more steps past the guy when he called out to Eddie, 'You were here yesterday morning, weren't you?'

Eddie reflexively spun around; the guy had put down the newspaper, stood up, and was holding out what looked like a badge.

'You saw the body, right?'

His shoulders sank, and it wasn't just

the weight of the notebooks in his back pack. 'Oh damn,' he said quietly.

'You're not in any kind of trouble,' Dan Lee said. 'But I really do need to talk to you.'

'I gotta get to work,' Eddie said nervously. 'I can't be late.'

Dan looked at his watch. 'As I figure it, you're a good fifteen minutes earlier than you were yesterday when you called in the murder victim. That's all the time I'm probably going to need.'

Eddie began to stammer a denial but then he stopped. This guy looked pretty smart; he clearly knew what had happened. And he did seem okay. Dan asked him his name and Eddie told him.

'Look, Eddie, I get that you didn't want to get involved. But can you just explain to me what you were doing here?'

'I work part-time at the Permanent Grind, up on the other side of the traffic circle. Five mornings a week before classes, starting at six. This is the easiest way for me to get there?'

Dan nodded. As he had figured, Eddie lived in the 'student ghetto,' apartments

58

and housing owned by the university, a little further down Pomeroy Avenue. It was about a half mile walk or bus ride to the university itself. In another couple of hours there would likely be a regular flow of students through the area.

'Were you with anybody yesterday morning, when you discovered the victim?'

'Uh-uh. I was by myself. Nobody else gets up this early? I wasn't really paying attention coming up the stairs, kinda like I was just now? I usually just have my head down and I'm listening to music or lost in thought?'

Dan smiled at the upward inflections. Seemed he had the right guy.

'All of a sudden I almost stumbled over the guy. Sometimes there's a homeless person sleeping up there? So I figured I'd just step around him. Then I saw . . . all this *blood!* And his eyes and mouth were wide open. It was like a slasher movie! It scared the hell out of me.'

'I bet it did. You did the right thing calling it in.'

'I almost didn't. I was so freaked out, I

couldn't think too straight for a while. I started back down the stairs. I don't know where I was going. Then I stopped and started to get rational.'

Dan nodded. He remembered the 911 call had said that the victim was 'up there.'

'Do you remember seeing anything else on the landing? Any other people around?'

'No. Nope. There was just me.'

'Nothing else on the stairs or the landing? You didn't pick anything up, accidentally kick anything?'

'Nothing. There was just him.'

'Then what did you do? Did you go back up the stairs?'

'Hell no! Go back up there? No way. I took the back route, up King Boulevard. I got to work a few minutes late.'

'Did you tell anybody about what you'd seen?'

'Just the other barista. I was scared to tell anybody, but she could see I was spazzed, you know?'

'You mean like crazy, like you were still a little nuts from what you'd seen?'

'Yeah, yeah. So I told her about it. But

nobody else. Well, I mighta told a couple of the guys back at the student co-op when I got home that night. Everybody told me I shouldn't say anything more about it.'

'Why did they tell you that?'

'If . . . it was like a gang killing or something? They'd come looking for me. They talk about stuff like that in the news all the time, and on TV shows and stuff. They got me worried that maybe I shouldn't have made the 911 call even.'

'Nobody's coming looking for you, Eddie. You did exactly the right thing.'

Eddie looked at his watch. 'Hey, I gotta get going to work.'

Dan laid a reassuring hand on Eddie's shoulder. 'Okay. I don't want to make you late. Do you mind if I walk with you and talk some more? I promise I won't let anyone see you talking with a detective, okay?'

The talk didn't yield much more except to convince Dan there was nothing more to Eddie's story. He stopped outside the Permanent Grind and let the uneasy young man go into his job.

* * *

Altuve was a small beach community about an hour down the coast, not far from higher-profile resort towns like Santa Cristina, but definitely less fashionable and therefore more affordable. It was a nice place for a retired police officer to be able to own a small but comfortable cottage. The beach was a block away but visible from the porch of Andy's place, and the day was just warming up enough, despite the typical overcast, for them to sit on his porch in comfortable chairs, sipping beers.

'Thanks for the early lunch,' Leon said. 'Appreciate your going to the trouble to grill burgers like that. And Kelsey made a real nice salad. Fennel and grapefruit . . . you folks are turning into real gourmets down here.'

'Well, it's not often we get you to come visit us,' Andy said, leaning back in his seat and stretching his legs out to rest on the porch bannister. He looked pretty good for his age. He still had a good head of hair, and the white creeping into his mustache looked more distinguished than elderly. 'Kelsey thought it might be a little early to offer you a beer, but I said you wouldn't turn me down.'

'Well, the sun's over the yardarm somewhere, right?' Leon proffered his tall green bottle in a toast.

'Truth to that.' Andy returned the salute. 'We'll be sure to feed you some pie and coffee before letting you drive home. Can't have an officer of the law getting a DUI.'

Leon thought back to long-past nights with Andy and other fellow officers that involved a fair amount more drinking than this, and smiled wryly. 'So how's the fishing?'

'Sometimes good, sometimes not. In fact I was back out on the boat all weekend.'

'Still got the Flatfoot? You and Kelsey?'

'Yep, same boat. Kelsey doesn't enjoy the boat anymore. Hasn't come with me in a long time. I take it out, down the central coast, moor up for the night and come back the next day. I think she enjoys the peace, not having me around getting bored and restless under foot.'

'Catch anything?'

'As a matter of fact, yeah. A bluefin, can you believe it? Kelsey said she'd clean it but hasn't gotten to it yet. It's in the freezer. If I'd known sooner you were coming, we coulda had it for lunch.'

Leon laughed. 'Burgers were just fine.'

They sat for a long minute, quietly looking out at the surf in the distance. There were only a couple of people and a dog running along the shore.

'So what's going on up there in the big city?'

Leon stretched and actually yawned. It was incredibly peaceful and relaxing. He could understand why Andy had retired here. 'All the usual. Never lets up. Lots of young kids coming up in the department. Too bad you're not on the force anymore. We could use you.'

Andy laughed. 'Yeah, well, I'm liking it down here in Altuve. Fact of the matter, not missing anything about the job. I'll take fishing and beachcombing over police work any day.' He watched a girl throw a Frisbee for her dog to chase into a crashing wave. 'So I'm thinking you had a reason to drive down here and visit me.'

'It's always good to see you, Andy. But let's just say I took advantage of an excuse to come see you and Kelsey.'

The two men continued to stare out towards the beach, not looking at each other.

'A couple detectives just pulled a curious case. Guy got shot the other night. Ex-con, just out of the joint. Two bullets in the chest, close range. And a mark left on his throat. Three slashes with a knife, like a Y.' He drew a capital letter Y in the air with his finger. 'Sound familiar?'

'Who was this guy, do you know?'

'Arthur Tobias.'

Andy nodded, rocking slightly in his chair. He knew the name. Leon knew he would. 'Where'd they find him?'

'The stairs at the Pomeroy tunnel.'

'Damn, I thought they were going to rip those down a year or so ago. I guess not.' Andy took another pull off his beer bottle and kept staring forward. 'Who caught the case, anybody I know?'

'Jilly Garvey, remember her?'

'Sure. Her hair still short and red?'

'It is.'

'Smart and tough. Good police, that girl. I remember her old partner, Reggie Martinez. He was legendary. Took a bullet a couple years ago, as I recall.'

'He did. Her new partner's a young guy named Lee.'

Andy heaved a deep sigh and leaned forward, resting his forearms on his knees. The silence grew heavy and the surf in the distance suddenly sounded louder.

'Three marks, you say. Like a Y.'

'Uh huh. Carved into the side of his neck. I don't think it's a coincidence, do you?'

'And this happened when?'

'Night before last. Actually early Monday morning.' He finally turned to look at Andy. 'I'm sorry to bring all this up. Dredging up lots of bad memories for you and for Kelsey. But I figured we needed to talk. You might be of some help.'

'Kelsey's not gonna hear about it.'

Leon nodded. 'Understood.'

Andy sighed once again. 'Sounds like

the boys are back. Maybe you'll find the rest of them.'

★ ★ ★

It was Tuesday mid-afternoon before Jilly heard from Mickey Kendrick in the Medical Examiner's office. Surprisingly, it came in the form of a telephone call.

'Well, Mickey, this is unexpected. Do you just want to hear my voice?'

'Always, but I thought I'd do you the courtesy of a call to fill you in on my preliminary report, which I'll be sending over to you shortly.' Over the receiver, his voice was even more monotone than in person.

'I appreciate that. What's up?'

'Pretty straightforward cause of death, just as figured: two slugs, .38 caliber, to the chest at close range. Both were found in the victim and have been sent to SID. The incisions on the throat appear to have been made by a pen knife or similar, which did not leave any kind of residue worth mentioning.'

'And?'

'Your vic had a number of healed fractures. He seems to have been in a lot of fights. There were some older fractures in his nose and cheekbones, going pretty far back, that weren't set or treated properly and that grew back not quite right.'

Jilly thought back to how Tobias had looked lying on the ground. He did have the look of a prizefighter who had lost a few rounds too many.

'So, no bruises or wounds that could have occurred last night?'

'Absolutely not. He'd had 'em all for some time.'

'Okay; so we can be pretty sure that Tobias didn't get into a fight that night, didn't put up a struggle with his killer, and our hypothesis has been enforced that he was either surprised or actually knew the shooter and didn't suspect anything.'

'That's your bailiwick, but, yes, the evidence would be consistent with those assumptions.'

Jilly thought that over. The guy got in a lot of fights throughout his life. That could mean a grudge existed. He was likely shot by someone he knew, and who knew him. That involved a lot of speculation, more than she ever felt comfortable with, but it was somewhere to start, at the very least.

There wasn't much more for Mickey to report, and after he told her to expect the preliminary in an email within the hour, she thanked him and rang off.

'Hey Jilly!' Dan called from his desk. 'You should come take a look at this!'

She walked behind him and leaned down to peer at his monitor. A somewhat high-contrast black and white video was playing on the screen.

'Do you believe this? I got footage!'

'From the stairs?'

'The foot of the stairs, at the tunnel! The camera was actually operating that night! Whenever a vehicle approaches the flashing caution light, it activates. Okay, so Tobias left the Albatross at approximately two in the morning . . . it took me less than ten minutes to walk to the circle yesterday, so figure he got to the stairs no earlier than 2:05. The killing could have gone down pretty quickly so I started looking at the footage from 2:10 and went forward.' Dan clicked and dragged the cursor across a slider at the bottom of the video, moving the action back. 'It was a long shot, but if there happened to be a car going by at the right moment . . . here, take a look at this!' He pointed to the time stamp at the bottom corner. It read 2:14. Then he pointed to the video itself, actually a series of still shots taken a second or so apart, which looked down on the front of a slowly approaching late model Ford. Despite the high contrast of darks and lights under the street lighting, the resolution was surprisingly good. The bottom of the stairway was vaguely visible in the background . . . and a small shadowed figure crossing Pomeroy Avenue right behind the car, likely coming directly from those stairs.

'Could that be our killer?' Dan asked.

'Could very well be. At the very least, we've got a person of interest. Can we get any better resolution on them?'

'The cams have gotten pretty good. I'd bet I could blow this up on the monitor.' Dan took a screen shot and opened it, enlarging it.

They both squinted at the image. 'Seems to be a woman,' Jilly said. 'Light trench coat, long dark hair, no hat. Can we sharpen this image any?'

'Not much I can do with it, I'm afraid. We could send it for forensic video analysis.'

Jilly sighed. 'And you know how long that's going to take.' Digital Image Forensics was one of the most in-demand and overworked agencies in the department.

'I hear you. But what's our alternative? This could be huge.'

'I've got an idea,' Jilly said. 'Give me a copy of this on a flash drive.'

★　★　★

Campbell J. Kasten ran a small post-production house dealing in contract video work from studios and television stations as well as the occasional out-of-town film director who was shooting in the area. There were good reasons he was always happy to see Jilly. He felt like he still owed her a favor or two.

71

When his receptionist announced Jilly, he strode out from the editing bay with a smile beaming through his considerable mountain-man beard. 'Detective, it's been too long! Always glad to see you!' He led her back to his small office and cleared some debris off a chair for her. 'Please forgive the mess around here. We're always so busy that we never get around to straightening up.'

'I was always told that a tidy office is the sign of getting nothing done.' Jilly smiled as she sat. Kasten followed suit, peering out at her from behind a monitor and a pile of paperwork on his desk.

'How's the family, Cam?'

'Everybody's great. Helen always tells me that if I should see you, to say hello and thanks again.'

'No thanks necessary. I've told you that. It was just our job.'

'Your job! You caught that guy on the way to *our house*! I can't bear to think of what might have happened, considering those other people . . . '

'Luckily he acted stupidly. There have been others like him, answering classified online ads that got away with theft and worse. This time we were able to track his patterns and identify him. But you know all that.'

Kasten shook his head. 'But the things he did to some of those people . . . '

'It's better not to dwell on things like that. It all worked out.'

'My daughters learned a lesson too. No more posting ads to sell their old electronic stuff, or anything else for that matter.' He shook his head and smiled. 'But that was a while ago, and I long ago took your advice and don't look back on that. So what can I do for you?'

Jilly pulled the flash drive stick out of her pocket. 'I was hoping you might be able to enhance the images on this so I can get some more detail from the background.'

He took the drive from her, uncapped it, and inserted it into a slot on his computer, tapping several keys and clicking his mouse as he peered at the screen intently. Finally he nodded and turned the screen so she could also see it.

'You mean this person back here?' He

used his mouse to twirl the cursor around part of the image he had brought up.

'Yeah. Any way it might be possible to get a better look at who they might be?'

He nodded, still staring at the monitor. 'I'd say so, yeah. We have software that can pull that up and extrapolate detail.' He looked up at her. 'It could have a high probability of accuracy, but you know I can't guarantee it.'

Jilly nodded back. 'I'm not concerned about using this as evidence. This isn't even an official request. I just need something to use as a jumping-off point.' She realized that for evidentiary concerns, she would still have to send a copy of the screen shots to Digital Image Forensics and wait until hell froze over to get confirmation, but she needed to get moving on this. This had to be off the books. Her gut feeling was that Kasten could be trusted. She looked at him intently. 'And this needs to be completely confidential. Can you personally do the work on this, and not show it to *anybody* else whatsoever?'

'Sure.'

'I can't ask you to rush this. I know

you've got your own workload. But can you give me an idea when you might be able to tell me if you've got anything?'

Kasten smiled again. 'How's a couple days sound?'

★ ★ ★

Jilly returned to the unit to find Leon and Dan standing by Dan's desk. They saw her and motioned for her to join them.

'What's up?'

'I was just about to find out. Leon says he's got something for us.'

'There are some things that might touch upon your Tobias case,' Leon said seriously.

'You seemed quite interested in it at the meeting,' said Jilly.

Leon nodded. 'As I said, there were things that definitely rang bells for me. But I had to check a few things before I felt okay telling you.'

Dan and Jilly said nothing but simply waited.

'I don't know whether you knew Andy Vernon. Back when I was a rookie in uniform, he was my training officer.'

'Sure,' said Jilly. 'I remember him. Big guy. They were scared of him on the street. Nobody messed with him.'

'That's him. Even I was afraid of him. As I got to know him, I found out he was a good man and a good cop. He taught me well. He lives down the coast in Altuve now, and I drove down to see him. I spent this morning having a long talk with him, getting the story right.'

'How's all this related to the Tobias case?'

'Andy had a son, named Drew. Smart guy, already big as his dad. Terrific athlete. He worked out, liked to box and did some mixed martial arts. Fourteen years ago, he got accepted at Hillside College down in Sycamore. Andy was proud as hell of him.'

'Oh my God,' said Jilly. 'I remember now. Not all the details, but I remember.'

Leon took a deep breath and stared down, hands on hips, before continuing. 'Good college, Hillside. In the *nice* part of Sycamore. You know what Sycamore's like.'

They all knew it well. Sycamore was a smaller city bordering their own. It had originally been a suburban town with upper-middle-class denizens, but over the years had grown and spread, as cities tend to do, and diversified. There was a remarkable leap of socioeconomic disparity, from the still lovely residences and the college campus in the hills to the east, to the seamier urban areas to the west, more or less symbolically separated by a major freeway and a cluster of railroad tracks. The 'nice' part of Sycamore was nice indeed. The 'dangerous' part was dangerous indeed, with an alarming rate of violent crime. A common joke had it that in the inner city of Sycamore, the beer trucks had tail gunners. While some homogenization was slowly occurring, it was still as if there were two separate cities included under the same municipal banner. It had to be a nightmare to govern and police.

"Drew decided he didn't want to live on campus but wanted to find an apartment and commute to classes. Andy wasn't too hot on the idea. As much as he tried to financially help him, he knew they couldn't afford for him to live near the school. But Drew was like his old man, stubborn and insistent. He said things were changing in parts of west Sycamore, and he'd found a place in a transitional neighborhood that was decent. He was going to get a part-time job and a roommate and he could swing it. So Andy went and checked out the apartment and the neighborhood. It was a small street called Yarnell. It was older but seemed to be going through some revitalization. There were small low-rise apartment houses, kinda like brownstones or town-houses. Some of them had been recently renovated to attract renters. Mostly it was still older neighbors, families. He figured Drew would do all right there. So he reluctantly gave his okay and cosigned the lease.

"Drew and his roommate started settling in. That's when Andy got his first surprise: Drew's roomie was a girl! His new girlfriend, in fact. That kind of threw Andy and his wife for a loop. He's kind of conservative. But they figured they'd work it out and get used to the idea. Like I said, Drew had a mind of his own.

"The girlfriend provided the only testimony about what happened, one night not long after they'd moved in. It was the evening to put out the garbage cans for pickup in the morning, the same kind of plastic wheeled bins that we have here. Drew saw some kids, teenagers, kicking his can over and spraying a gang symbol on the side of it, so he yelled at them and chased them away. He figured that was the end of that. But it wasn't.

'Later that night, Drew heard noises and went outside to find his car had been spray painted, the windows and the doors, the same gang sign as on the trash can. He must have gone after them and confronted them. When he came back to the apartment, he told the girlfriend about the car and said he'd made sure they knew not to come around anymore. He planned to call the police in the morning. They went back to sleep and that seemed to be the end of it.'

At this point, Jilly knew what was coming and waited with apprehension. All of this was a new story to Dan and he listened with no idea of the tragic climax.

'The girlfriend must have slept soundly after that. She didn't wake up until early the next morning. She couldn't find Drew so she figured he had headed off to class. She found his body on the steps of the building. He'd been shot twice at close range . . . and that same gang symbol had been cut with a knife into his neck.' Leon stared at the two detectives. 'I'm guessing you can figure out what that symbol was. That's right. Not a pinwheel. The letter Y, for Yarnell Street.' He traced it into the air. 'Eighteen years old, Andy's only kid. Dead and gone.'

'What happened after that?' asked Dan. 'Did they bring in the gang kids?'

'Negative. There were three kids who came up on the radar. Lots of people in the neighborhood knew who they were. They were all around maybe sixteen to nineteen. One got picked up but they couldn't find the other two. Their families claimed to have no idea where they'd gone. The first kid they had to let go. Insufficient evidence. That kid lit out as soon as he was free. They all disappeared.'

'But the gang symbol,' Jilly said. 'The Y or whatever it was.'

'The DA said it was insufficient. There was no history of that ever having been used by any gang in the area. Nobody could claim to have ever seen it before that night. There was no clear chain to connect them to it. Nobody had witnessed the confrontations; there was just the girlfriend's secondhand hearsay about what had happened. Anybody could have done it, they said. And nobody ever came forward who could positively ID anybody involved. The little scumbags were never even charged, and after a half-hearted attempt to find them, they gave up.'

'But it was the son of a cop,' said Dan. 'That must have been some motivation for the investigators!'

Leon shrugged. 'You'd think.' He didn't say it but his look conveyed the sentiment: *it's Sycamore*.

'That must have been horrible for Andy and his wife,' said Jilly.

'It killed something inside both of them. I don't think they've ever recovered.'

81

'And you say the kids disappeared after that?'

'Went off the scope completely. Andy reached out to people he knew in the Sycamore PD, hired private investigators, the whole nine yards, but they were gone without a trace. The youngest kid turned up a couple years later as soon as he'd reached that magic age when he could be tried as an adult; went and got himself arrested and won a good long sentence at a state institution. You might have guessed the punch line by now. The young one was Arthur Tobias, your vic.'

Jilly and Dan were still processing that when Leon added, 'If it's all right with the both of you, I'd like to help you out on this one. I think you understand.'

Jilly leaned over the desk, tapping her fingers on the surface for several beats, before looking up and answering. 'Leon, I've got some concerns about you coming in on this. You've clearly got a personal interest in the case. I'm not sure you can be objective. You could jeopardize every-thing.'

'Jilly, I have to be in on this. I know

things that can help. I can keep it separated.'

'Andy's your friend. He was your training officer. This involves the men who killed his son. It's personal.'

'I won't let it be personal. My interest is in clearing your case. If it happens that it helps clear the older case, so much the better.'

Jilly and Dan exchanged a look. It was clear that Dan was going to follow her lead on the decision. She knew Leon much better than he did. She ticked off a list in her head: they could definitely use another pair of legs to cover the actual physical ground that this one would demand, and she knew Leon as one of the most principled members of not just Personal Crimes but the whole department.

She sighed deeply. 'At the first sign of trouble, I'm going to kick you off this,' she said, eyeing Leon seriously. 'Anything that might prevent an apprehension *and* conviction.'

'Agreed,' Leon replied, equally serious.

'And we're going to have to run this by Castillo.'

Leon nodded again, this time more hesitantly. Jilly continued.

'What are the odds that Andy's mixed up in this?'

He shook his head vigorously. 'No way. More likely the original Yarnell Street boys, or someone connected to them, might have surfaced again to settle some old score. In any case, I promise you my primary focus will be this case. Anything that turns up that sheds some light on what happened to Drew, and maybe turns up the rest of the perps, will be icing on the cake.'

Leon Simpkins, easily the most loquacious and persuasive detective in Personal Crimes when he wished to be, was also kiddingly known as Likable Leon among his colleagues. He needed most of those skills of persuasion in Lieutenant Hank Castillo's office alongside Jilly and Dan. After making their case and answering a number of Castillo's misgivings, they stood silently before his desk, waiting for him to make his judgment.

Castillo sighed deeply and eyed Simpkins carefully. 'Leon, I want something understood. This case involves the murder of

Arthur Tobias. You are not investigating the murder of Drew Vernon.'

'Understood, Lou.'

'I'm allowing this because I'm worried this could foreshadow more violence, Garvey and Lee are going to need extra footwork, and you can maybe contribute some insights into their investigation because of what you know. Your own history suggests I can trust you to exercise proper judgment. Don't disappoint me.'

'I won't.'

'I can't let you neglect your own caseload with your own partner for more than a few days. Give it what you can, but next week I'm handing it all back to Garvey and Lee.'

'Thanks, Lou. I'll try not to leave Art high and dry this week either. I'll work with Dan and Jilly mornings and get back to our own table in the afternoons.'

'Good luck.' Castillo looked down at his ever-present paperwork, then glanced up, eyebrows raised, surprised that they were still there. 'Anything else?'

★ ★ ★

Art Dowdy sat way back in his chair, looking very tired indeed, and stared up at Leon.

'So you're thinking that the murder of Andy Vernon's kid is somehow connected with this?'

'It can't be a coincidence. If you want to stay clear of this one, I'm okay with that. But I can't let it rest. He was one of the guys that probably killed Drew and then disappeared. Maybe the others are involved in his own shooting.'

Dowdy sighed in resignation. He knew his partner well; when he got his teeth into something he was like a pit bull. He wasn't about to open his jaws. 'Let me know if you need any help. I can handle this stuff okay.' He gestured at two fairly thick folders on his desk. 'Piece of cake.'

'I'll fit this in and work on our caseload in the afternoons. You know I won't leave you hanging.'

Dowdy smiled wryly. 'Go get 'em, Leon. I hope to hell something comes out of this that can give Andy some closure.'

'You and me both,' Leon replied. 'You and me both.'

4

By the time Jilly arrived at work, Dan was already deep into a conversation on his phone, waving to her. A few moments later he hung up the receiver with an exhalation.

'So much for phone calls to Wentworth. Most of my calls got shuttled around from one jammed-up official to another. I spoke with the officer who was in charge of preparing Tobias for parole. He was considered a model prisoner, stayed out of trouble, had a few jobs like the prison laundry and so forth. He kept his nose down and didn't associate with other prisoners very much. He was very cooperative with the parole guy and everything went smoothly. The Catholic chaplain, though, is interested in having us come sit down with him. It seems that he's one person that Tobias did spend a lot of time with, and confided in.'

Jilly recalled the rosary beads in

Tobias's pocket. 'Were you able to talk with him?'

'Only briefly. Everybody there sounds overwhelmed. He said he could see us tomorrow. So I guess we're making a trip out to Wentworth. But he did say there's a lot he can tell us, so I think it's worth it. Uh, what's that I'm hearing? More of your classical music?'

'Oh. New ringtone on my phone. Haydn's *Surprise Symphony*.' She pulled out the phone, stabbed the answer button and said, 'Garvey.' A few seconds later, after a terse conversation, she stabbed it again.

'That was Leon. He's in Sycamore, checking out what he can find on the Drew Vernon murder case angle. He'll try to connect up with us in person later today, but he also has to jump back on his caseload with Art.'

'Got a full plate, that man.'

'Don't we all. But it's important to him to have a hand in this case too.'

'You're sure you're okay with him following up on this particular aspect of the case?'

'He's the logical one to do it. I've known Leon for a long time and I trust him. He's a good investigator and a good man. He knows he's got limits.'

'Still . . . you and I both know that an investigator shouldn't be working on something where he's personally involved. It could affect his judgment.'

'I'm not asking him for judgment. I'm asking him for whatever information he can gather. I'm still the lead on this. Anything he gets, he's got to bring to me.'

'Okay, Jilly. You know I trust your instincts.'

Jilly sighed to herself. She hoped she trusted them as implicitly as her partner did.

★   ★   ★

Sycamore PD Detective Roy Truax was looking his age, with thinning hair and a growing gut, but he had retained an unmistakable intensity. Leon felt right at home in the small bare-bones interview room; it would have fit right in with his own squad.

'Drew Vernon: that was your case, right?' Leon was asking.

'Yep. My gold badge was fairly new then. My partner took lead on that case. But how could I forget it?' Truax shook his head, remembering his partner. 'Bobby Valenzuela. Mean, unorthodox, but a decent detective. May he rest in peace.'

There didn't seem to be many individuals left at Sycamore PD who had a personal memory of the case. A lot had happened in the intervening years. People transferred, left, died. It was that kind of city and that kind of department.

'What can you tell me about the case?'

'I can tell you we never solved it. We had some ideas but nothing panned out. It was a cop-related death; we took that very seriously.'

'So you must have gone all out on this. What went wrong?'

'Everything.'

'Walk me through it?'

'When we first got there that morning, all we knew was a young guy, a kid really, was shot twice in the chest point-blank.

And he had this mark stabbed into the side of his throat, like a big Y.' Truax made the letter in the air with his finger. 'Nearby there was a garbage can with the same figure spray painted on it. And a car, the victim's. Same thing, big spray painted Ys. We figured some new gang maybe: Y like for Yarnell Street? Nobody ever matched it with any known gang tags anywhere. The dead kid didn't look like a gangbanger. He was clean-cut, in a Hillside College windbreaker. Then we learned he was a student and the son of a cop from your department.'

'There was a girlfriend, I understand.'

'Yeah, she was the one who found the body and called it in. We looked into her, of course, and decided she was in the clear. She said that the vic had yelled at some guys on the street who were vandalizing their garbage cans, and then they came back and tagged his car. He went back out to confront them again and ran them off, apparently with physical force.'

'Do you remember the girlfriend's name?'

'That was so long ago. I have it in the file; I can pull it from records for you. Asian kid is all I remember, around eighteen. Glasses. Nerdy, studious type.'

'Did she have parents or family around?'

'She was from out of town, as memory serves. No family around here.'

'And nothing in past cases about someone carving something like that in the neck of the victim?'

Truax shook his head. 'Nothing like it ever. We checked all the nearby gang units and task forces for the sign. Nobody had ever seen anything like it, not graffiti or tats or anything resembling it. We couldn't connect it with any clique or set.'

'Never found the gun?'

'Nope. Cheap five-shot revolver. The bullets yielded nothing.'

'Witnesses?'

'An old lady across the street had looked out her window when she heard the shots and saw three guys running away. She couldn't identify any of them. All she knew was they were 'dark shapes'. If there were other wits, they were scared to get involved.'

'And the earlier confrontations you mentioned, nobody witnessed them either?'

'Same deal. Nobody came forward.'

'So who were your suspects?'

'A couple of knuckleheads from the street that Bobby had heard about. We brought one of them in and couldn't find the other. There was also a younger kid that had been seen in their company. We tried to run him down as well, but he was gone too. I remember talking to his mother. Sheesh! The aroma was like touring a brewery. She didn't know what day it was, much less where her burdensome little boy was. She couldn't even remember when she last saw him. A sloppy drunk, kept going off on emotional tangents about her lot in life.'

Leon steered him back on point. 'Younger kid, like maybe sixteen or so? Big kid? That must have been Tobias.'

'Yeah, that was him. The other two were maybe nineteen, no longer juvies. No major beefs, yet, but the signs were there . . . they were definitely headed for trouble. We figured what's his name, Tobias, was like a tag-along, a wannabe. He'd make it a trio of losers. This wasn't exactly a conclave of brain surgeons, judging by the one we brought in. You could tell he was destined for great things, all right.'

'You must have searched all the homes anyway.'

'Sure. All right there on Yarnell. The one guy, the one we brought in, lived with his parents. The other guy, turned out he lived by himself in a cheap walk-up flat, no family. Didn't even lock up when he fled. We searched all three homes. Found nothing that would've helped. Never found the gun.'

'No prints or trace to be found at the scene?'

'Nada. SID went over it really well. No usable prints on the cans or the car, except the victim's. The medical examiner was able to tell us pretty much the exact size and shape of the blade that was cut into the vic's throat but we never found any kind of blade to match.'

Leon sat in deep thought for a few beats. 'Anything else about the autopsy? I understand Drew might have gotten into a fight with the kids. Any chance of any traceable DNA on him, anything?'

'His knuckles were bruised. He'd gotten quite a few hits in to someone, most likely to the face since there was blood, but it didn't match up to anybody in the databases. But remember, that was fourteen, fifteen years ago. The tech was good but not as good as it is now. The guy we brought in to question didn't have any bruises consistent with a fight. We took a blood sample from him and it didn't match the blood on the victim's knuckles.'

'You said there were no bruises consistent with a fight. Does that mean the suspect had bruises of other sorts?'

Truax shrugged. 'There may have been. It'd all be in the file. I can have it pulled and send you copies.'

'That'd be a big help, thanks.' Leon's mind raced. 'How about the spray paint itself? That didn't lead anywhere, I'm guessing.'

'Oh, we tried that angle too. If we could've just found a can of spray paint in any of their homes, it would've been tenuous but at least it would've been something. There was never a single thing to connect any of them to it.' Truax stared across the table at Leon. 'We knew it was them. We just couldn't prove anything.'

'And there were never any other suspects?'

Truax shook his head. 'We did due diligence, tried every angle. But in our hearts we knew we had the right guys and lost them.'

'Did you learn that Tobias had surfaced a couple years later and was arrested for grand theft?'

'No, I didn't know until you told me about it today. You know how this grand system works. Sometimes the left hand and the right hand aren't talking. It was a couple years later, you said? We had moved on to other cases. This one had become cold and it was no longer on our radar.'

'You've got a cold case squad, right? They weren't interested in this one?'

'Not yet, I guess. They would've gotten to this one eventually, since it was important. But I don't have to tell you how many cold cases there are.'

Leon simply nodded. His own department had literally hundreds, and at any given time any assigned investigator would be looking at stacks of files.

'So you've never found out anything about the other two guys? There was never any sure conclusion?'

Truax pursed his lips grimly. 'We *were* sure. We couldn't prove anything legally unless we could have apprehended them, but we were 99.99 percent sure those knuckleheads were our guys. What we couldn't do was find them.'

Leon said nothing, not wanting to alienate the one lead he had from the original case, but something bothered him. It seemed to him that due diligence had *not* been at work. He knew all manner of factors entered into a detective's day-to-day decisions on whether to vigorously pursue a case, and he wondered if other circumstances, innocent or otherwise, could have distracted them. If he could keep on Truax's good side, he'd have the original case files to examine at some point. But that wasn't a sure thing. If the Sycamore detective copped an attitude and decided to make life hard for him, he might never see them. It was a job for Likable Leon.

Leon asked a few more softball questions and thanked Truax for his help. He promised that if his investigation turned up either of the other two Yarnell Street suspects, he'd include him in.

'I'll just pass it on to Cold Case,' Truax said matter-of-factly. 'But thanks.'

★   ★   ★

Neighborhoods, Leon considered, really do change. West Sycamore was apparently no exception.

There was not much left of Yarnell Street that would have been familiar to those who had lived there fourteen years earlier. The entire street was only three short blocks long, and Leon had now walked back and forth its entire length twice. Newer buildings occupied locations where older apartment houses had once stood: a pizza takeout, a vegan café, a vintage clothing store, two pet grooming shops, and three coffee houses. A handful of old brownstones still stood along one side of one block, but progress and gentrification had changed them as surely as it had the rest of the street.

Younger families, bearded fathers and tattooed mothers walking dogs and toddlers seemed everywhere. Late model SUVs lined the streets. Leon had found one elderly lady who had been there for over fourteen years, and she had little memory of anyone that might have been of any help to him. He knew that there were still sections of Sycamore where it wasn't safe to walk, day or night, or even wait for a train. This section of town had clearly become a wholehearted part of the 'safe' side of town, but it had also adopted a very different demographic from how it had once been. To where, he wondered, had the working-class people, the former inhabitants of Yarnell Street, been transplanted now?

He stopped once again in front of 2401 Yarnell. It was one of the few older structures that had been allowed to remain standing. Leon figured it was because these buildings had already been retrofitted and renovated, back when the gentrification had begun, to attract higher-paying tenants: subdivided into smaller apartments from the earlier family units. That was probably how Drew and his girlfriend had been able to get into one of them.

He stared down at the street. This was where Drew Vernon had been shot and his body found. Yarnell was narrow; he closed his eyes and could envision how it looked back then.

There was nothing here that could help him. If any answers actually existed, they'd lie within the case file of Drew Vernon's murder.

The strains of an alto sax melody broke his reverie. His phone's ringtone. It was Dowdy.

'We got a floater. You available?'

'Sure. Tell me where to meet you.'

'You can't miss it. Head for the fishing pier and follow your nose.'

★   ★   ★

Les Lonergan was halfway to the sidewalk from the porch of Arlo Merchant's house when he saw Dan approaching.

'Just the man I was looking for,' Dan said.

'You again. Now what?'

'Les, I just need you to explain something for me. You didn't tell us that you spent some of your time at Wentworth.'

'Wentworth? I was there for less than a year. They transferred me from Presa Vista to finish up my time. So what?'

'So did you know Arthur Tobias when you were there?'

Lonergan looked genuinely surprised. 'He was at Wentworth? I . . . no! I didn't know him!'

'You told us he looked familiar.'

'Yeah, maybe I saw him there. That might be it. But there's a lot of cons at Wentworth. I didn't know him.'

'I think we need to talk some more, Les.'

'Look, I'm trying to get to work! I can't lose this job! I'm not the one you should be bugging about all this!'

'What do you mean?'

'I mean you need to ask Sammy about

this. He told you he didn't talk with Tobias . . . but he did! He had a couple, three conversations with him. And last Sunday, I saw him walk out the door after Tobias!'

'Wait a minute! You saw them go out last Sunday night? Together?'

'Yeah. Sorta. He followed him out the door, anyway.'

'Why didn't you say anything about this the other day when we were here?'

'Come on! I'm not gonna rat out a guy, especially not right in front of him! But if you're looking at me for something, that's different. I got nothing to do with this, I swear. Sammy's the guy you need to be talking to. He probably knows more about Tobias than he was letting on.'

'So where's Sammy now?'

'I don't know. Maybe at work. I haven't seen him around the house but maybe he's around there. Arlo can tell you. I swear, I didn't know the Tobias guy! Can I go now?'

Merchant was indeed in the house, and said he hadn't seen Figueroa all day. He just assumed he was at work.

Dan wondered how this guy's house ever got into the system. He told Merchant to contact him the minute Figueroa returned.

5

Falcon Island would sound like a lovely place if someone were unaware that it was the site of one of the state's most formidable maximum security prisons. There was little else on the small island, in fact, but sheer jagged tree-topped cliffs that were home to the isle's namesake bird. Anyone clever enough to escape the prison itself would have to contend with a tortuous descent to the coast and then deal with the ferocious rip tides in order to get to the mainland. It was a facility that had seen few breakouts in its history. This was the home of Mikal Leviev and Billy Hayworth, the accomplices of Arthur Tobias, and the destination of Leon Simpkins on his Thursday morning drive up the coast.

He had already been informed that Hayworth was in the prison infirmary and unavailable to be interviewed, but Leviev had agreed to meet with him. A burly guard led Mikal Leviev into the meeting room and seated him in a heavy wooden chair across the table from Leon. He was lean and muscular, with ropy arms covered with tattoos, a shaved head, squinty dark eyes under hooded eyebrows, and the nasty scowl Leon knew from so many lifetime losers. The guard stood against the wall, keeping a close eye on the inmate.

Leviev glared up and down at Leon for a long time as the detective waited him out, returning his laser gaze with a serene stare. It was a technique he had perfected over the years; Leon was a patient man. Long periods of silence didn't bother him but, he had learned, it usually put others ill at ease, which was to his advantage.

Finally Leviev spoke, in a deep basso rumble. 'So the kid got scrubbed. I figure that must be why you're here to see me?'

Volunteering information from the get-go. Surprising. 'So you know about that. News travels fast,'

Leviev shrugged. 'You'd be surprised *how* fast.'

'Just to be perfectly clear, you are

talking about Arthur Tobias, correct?'

Leviev nodded. 'Baby Huey. The kid.'

'Baby Huey?'

'Yeah, we had these really old comic books and there was this character, a gigantic dumb baby duck or something, named Baby Huey. So we called him that. It's the kid.'

'Okay. You don't sound surprised that someone killed him.'

Leviev shrugged again, a small smile playing on the corners of his mouth. 'Stuff happens.'

'I don't suppose you have any idea who or why.'

Leviev raised his hands and looked around him, almost comically. 'Well, I sure didn't do it, and Billy, he's up in the infirmary with a lotta stitches. I guess it wasn't us.'

'Your pal Billy got himself cut up good in a fight, I understand.'

'It happens. Sometimes the service in this resort is sub-standard, you know?'

Leon returned his own easy, amused smile. 'Mikal, maybe I'm smarter than the average detective, since I sure as hell already knew it wasn't you or Billy. I thought maybe you might know something about who else should be on my card.'

'I haven't seen him in, like, eleven years now. The kid was at Wentworth, right? Shouldn't you be looking at the friends he made there?'

Leon let the silence fall as he simply stared at the convict before resuming.

'Tell me something about when you knew him, back in Midland City.'

'What's to tell? Not like we were besties. We pulled a job together . . . allegedly.'

'You can go with 'alleged' job if you like, but I heard they pretty much followed you home from it. I've also been led to believe you three pulled some other jobs before that brilliant score that earned you all these long vacations. You must have known something about him. You had to have hung out together somewhat.'

Leviev grunted a laugh. 'Huey was a dork. A big, stupid dork. Pretty useful sometimes. I wouldn't exactly say he had *skills*. But he was big and strong and scary. And simple. He'd do what you needed and you didn't have to worry about him getting smart ideas about crossing you up. Good guy to have with you in a bar . . . or wherever.'

'Or wherever. Allegedly.' Leon nodded, never taking his eyes off Leviev. 'Just curious, by the way, why you were so willing to see me today.'

Another shrug. 'Something to break up the day. Not like I got a demanding schedule, you know? Plus, I love to waste a cop's time. Nothing I can tell you is gonna be any help since I don't know anything.'

'You're not worried the word's going to get out around here that you talked to me?'

Leviev slowly shook his head, also never breaking the staring contest.

Leon considered: *This guy's got all day, but I don't.*

'How long did you know Tobias?'

'I dunno; a year maybe. We didn't have an anniversary dinner, exchange presents, anything like that.'

'How'd you guys meet?'

'When you're looking for certain kinds of work, you kinda find each other.'

'He was a lot younger than you and Hayworth. In fact he was probably still a juvie when you first worked together. I'm thinking you thought he'd be handy to take a rap if you got caught. Juvies get off easy.'

The inmate's eyebrows raised slightly. 'Wow. Good thinking. You'd make a great criminal mastermind, you know? Always thought there's not much difference between police and *criminals*.' He punched the final word with irony.

'What else do you know about him? Did he have friends, family? Maybe a girlfriend?'

Leviev laughed outright. 'A girlfriend? Huey? Friends? He was a loner. Like I said, he was a dork.'

'So I guess you and Tommy were his only friends and family? Lucky guy.'

'Hey, we looked out for him. The kid mostly lived on the street, had a string of dead-end jobs, you know, like flipping burgers and asking 'Do you want fries with that? Supersize your order?' He

109

might have gotten in *real* trouble if not for us. We helped him out with a few bucks here and there, made sure he didn't starve or get killed by saying the wrong thing to the wrong guy.'

'Tobias did that a lot, did he?'

'You know, it's usually the little guys you gotta watch out for, right? Like, the really big guy isn't gonna come up to you in a bar and try to show off for a girl or to make himself feel any bigger. It's always the half-pint Napoleon who wants a piece of you, no matter how big you are.'

Leon nodded.

'Not the case with Huey. He was as big as Godzilla and not as pretty, but he had issues. Always felt like he was trying to stay low but he couldn't resist facing down some fool now and then. Too sensitive.'

'He got in a lot of fights, did he?' Leon thought about what Jilly had told him about the coroner's report and Tobias's old healed fractures.

'I wouldn't say a lot. Most of the time he'd intimidate the other guys, seeing's how he was so big and creepy, with that messed-up face. But there was always the one who wouldn't back down. Or the two or three. Huey wasn't very heedful of the numbers. One time he mouthed off and threw down to three guys at once. They beat him down good. We had to back them down, take him to the ER and make up some stories about what happened. So I'm not kidding, we probably saved his life more than once. We also kept him out of the police's view, got him out of places before he could get picked up. We were like his guardian angels, man.'

Leon considered that Tobias had no police record in Midland City prior to the big job. Somehow he had remained inconspicuous despite his propensity for trouble. Unlikely guardian angels indeed.

'Was there anybody in Midland City that he knew from Sycamore? Anybody ever show up from those days looking for him?'

'Sycamore. That where he was from? No idea. Far as I know, like I said, he didn't have nobody from nowhere.'

'You were just talking about keeping him from saying the wrong thing to the wrong guy. Maybe you were remiss in your duties at some point.'

'Whattaya mean?'

'Any chance someone had a grudge against him from Midland City, who would have kept tabs on him up to now?'

Leviev shook his head and squinted at Leon. 'Have you been listening? He wasn't worth it. He never did anything important enough for anyone to remember him for a week, much less years.'

'Just curious, then: any thought as to why he got himself killed?'

Leviev shrugged. 'I'm guessing when he got out, he popped his mouth off to the wrong hothead. Like I said: stuff happens.'

Leon nodded. He pulled a piece of paper out of his pocket and placed it on the table in front of Leviev. He had drawn the three-pronged Y on it.

'Ever see this before, written anywhere, maybe the sign of a crew or something?'

The convict stared at the paper impassively, then looked back up at Leon. 'Nope. What is it?'

'It was cut into him as a calling card.'

'Huh. How about that.'

'So it means nothing to you?'

'Just that there are some crazy fools out there. But I knew that.'

There wasn't much more to the conversation. The short remainder of the interview convinced Leon that Tobias' life in Midland City had been lonely and tedious. The best he could manage for friends were two considerably older career criminals that didn't really think that much of him either. He had hung around in Midland City long enough to get an education from Leviev and Hayworth that put him on the path to his destruction. Maybe Leviev was holding something back, but Leon's gut told him no.

As he began the long drive back down the coast, he reflected that it had been basically a waste of most of his morning, something Leviev had gleefully enjoyed. Maybe there were answers at Wentworth. He hoped Jilly and Dan were having better luck there.

*   *   *

Leon found himself back in the squad room ahead of Dan and Jilly. He hoped that meant their trip to Wentworth was fruitful. Dowdy was headed out and they met near Leon's desk.

'How's it going, Art?'

'Looks like they pulled a match on the floater. He was in the system. Lucky us. They're sending over ID this afternoon. Maybe it'll be a break.'

'That would be nice. Bearing up without me?'

'I'd say in some ways it's easier,' Dowdy deadpanned. 'I hope you're making headway with Garvey and Lee.'

'I wish I could say I was, but so far I'm spinning my wheels. The Lou's only going to allow me a couple more days on this anyway. I don't know, maybe it'll all be in vain. So you can look forward to having me all to yourself again next week.'

'Fortunate me. You better hope I don't get too used to being a solo act.'

'Just for the mornings. I need to have a sit-down with Jilly and Dan when they get back, get us all on the same page — but then I'll jump back in with you the rest of today.'

Dowdy nodded. 'By the way, there's a

package on your desk.' He jerked his thumb over his shoulder and headed for the stairs.

There was indeed a large sturdy manila envelope addressed to Leon that had apparently been delivered by messenger from Sycamore PD. He unwound the red string around the clasp and then opened the sealed flap. Truax had come through, and in record time.

There were photocopied pages of the case file on Drew Vernon, including photos. Leon sat down and began to page through them. At first he simply scanned, looking for salient information, but he soon found himself reading carefully.

The reports were consistent with everything that Truax had described. There were photos of the body on the stairs, the graffiti sprayed on the garbage can and car. He peered at the close-ups of the three-pronged Y on the victim's throat. It looked almost exactly like the mark left on Arthur Tobias.

Drew's girlfriend's name was Mary Evelyn Cho. In her statement she had indicated that her closest family, including her parents, resided in Denver, Colorado. They had originally lived near Sycamore, where she had met Drew the year before while finishing high school. When her parents had moved, she had remained to attend Hillside College and be with Drew, with whom she had become romantically involved.

And most of this, thought Leon, unknown to Andy. But he reminded himself that was not his focus. He was looking for anything that would give a clue to what happened to Tobias, why that emblem had carried over to his own murder so many years later.

Arthur Tobias, aged sixteen. The name was there with the other suspects: Reuben Serazin, who went by the name Rudy; and Nestor Lowell, both nineteen. The only one of the three who had been apprehended for questioning was Serazin. The report of their interview with him noted that aside from some slight discoloration around his neck that they deemed inconsequential, he had no abrasions, wounds, or other signs of having been in a recent serious fight. He consented to have blood drawn before he was released but it had not turned out to be a match to any of the evidence from the crime scene.

Tobias, who lived with his mother, and Lowell, who lived on his own, were never located. According to Lowell's employer, a local diner, he never showed up for his kitchen job again and had even left a paycheck behind.

Leon had a feeling it wouldn't do much good, but at least now he had names to go on. He opened the browser on his computer and began some internet searches to see if he could find something . . . anything.

Both Reuben Serazin and Nestor Lowell were complete dead ends. He found nothing on either one of them after the date of their disappearance. His search unearthed birth records, and in Serazin's case a baptismal record, all from Sycamore. That also allowed him to derive parental names that led to similar dead ends. Serazin's father and mother had lived on Yarnell Street but were both now deceased. Shortly after Lowell had been born, his father had been incarcerated and seemed to have spent the overwhelming majority of his time since then, including at present, as a guest of the state in various penal institutions. Lowell's mother did not even come up in searches.

He wasn't sure why he searched her out, but he did locate a Mary Evelyn Cho in the Denver area. He couldn't believe there were all that many Mary Evelyns, much less surnamed Cho, so he felt confident he had found the right one. He just wasn't sure how that would be of any help, but she seemed to be the only link he had to the murderers, as tenuous as it was, so he made note of it all. He sighed, hoping that Dan and Jilly were finding more clarity at Wentworth.

★   ★   ★

In contrast to the wild, remote setting of Falcon Island, Wentworth State Prison was grey and utilitarian, located at the northern end of the state's arid central valley. A visitor would have no illusions as to its purpose or personality.

Father Anthony Grabys was probably

in his early forties, but the high forehead caused by his receding blond hair made him look somewhat older. He spoke seriously, in a soft voice that still carried the accent of his native Lithuania. His pale blue eyes registered deep concern as he sat and spoke with Jilly and Dan about Arthur Tobias.

'I appreciate you came out to see me today. I know it's something of a drive.'

'We should thank you for your willingness to assist us,' said Jilly. 'It sounds as if you knew Arthur fairly well. We haven't found anybody else who can tell us much about him.'

'When I heard what had happened to him, I was deeply shaken. I had been waiting for word from him once he got settled. I believe he was sincere in his desire to start a new life. I don't understand how something like this could have happened.'

'We're trying to figure it out too, Father. So you don't have any idea who could have done this to him?'

'There was nobody who had it in for him?' Dan added. 'Somebody here at the prison, maybe?'

The priest shook his head, looking bewildered. 'Arthur kept to himself largely here. He hardly interacted with any of the others at all. I think it's possible I'm the only one he ever had any regular extended conversations with.'

'How did that first start,' Jilly asked, 'his coming to confide in you?'

'His self-examination began sometime in his second year here. He was trying to keep his head down and do his own time, as they say in here. It was difficult, perhaps because he was such a big man, and he had somewhat of a temper. He had to stand his ground and fight several times. There were signs it might turn into a problem; he knew his best interests lay in staying out of trouble but he had, it would seem, a propensity to fight. Then he had the visitor.'

'Visitor?'

'Yes. When he first came to see me, he said there had been someone who had asked to see him, a minister of some sort. I'm not even sure if it was someone he knew or just a stranger on a mission who picked him out at random. I never learned exactly what was said to him, but Arthur said it had convinced him to re-examine his life and made him determined to change.'

'Did this minister ever return to talk with him again?'

'No, I don't think so. And to my knowledge, he had no other visitors in all his time here. There was just that one man.'

'That's pretty unusual,' Dan said.

'Yes, it was. But it somehow made Arthur want to talk further to someone. He said he never found anyone in the inmate population he could trust. So he sought me out and, after he decided he could talk freely with me, we met every week for about an hour and just talked.'

'For around nine years, every week?'

'For the most part. There were weeks I wasn't here, and I took a six-month sabbatical a few years back, but he almost always kept our weekly appointment when I was able to. He wouldn't talk to anybody else. I think he had a general suspicion of religion and thus of most clergy members.'

'These talks,' Dan said. 'Were these, like, confessions?'

'I regarded them as such. He told me very serious things. He was desperate for some kind of redemption but couldn't bring himself to trust the only ultimate solutions I could offer. I urged him to embrace the sacraments and to face the responsibility for what he had done. Perhaps he would have done so. I pray he found peace with himself and absolution from God before he died.'

'Redemption,' repeated Jilly. 'He had a huge burden of guilt of some kind.'

Grabys nodded.

'These things he told you about, Father . . . are they things you can share with us? It sounds as if you judged the seal of the confessional applied.'

'For a long time, I treated it as such, even if it wasn't technically a sacramental confession. Had his disclosure come during the administration of the sacrament of penance, it would be inviolable even after his death. But I didn't administer the sacrament, and I decided there's a greater good here to be addressed, to find the person who took his life. I'm deeply worried about the possibility that he died before he could make his peace and save his soul. Do you think that someone in his earlier life, before he came here, was responsible for his death?'

'Yes, we think that's very much a possibility.'

'Then I've determined to tell you as much of his story as I know, in hopes it will guide you. You're the only ones who'll make the effort to bring justice to everyone who deserves it.'

And to the amazement of Dan and Jilly, the solemn priest began to tell them the detailed story of the young Arthur Tobias.

6

It was one of those heavily overcast early evenings when the air was wet and cold and heavy. There was almost a tangible depression in the atmosphere weighing upon people beginning to leave work by car, train or bus, impelling them to scurry home as quickly as possible to someplace warm and welcoming for the remains of the day.

The teenager hustling down the street in his hoodie, a canvas backpack slung over his shoulder, wouldn't have understood that sentiment. 'Home' was something to avoid returning to. It wasn't like there would be a hot dinner or a mug of cocoa and a loving smile waiting for him. His mother had started drinking several hours ago and was already well in the bag. She had started in on another incoherent rant against his long-gone father that had then turned against him. Right after he had slammed the door of the apartment on his way out, she had probably curled up on the couch and passed out.

Toby walked down the littered sidewalk of Yarnell Street, avoiding eye contact with anyone at the bus stop or on the stoops of the brownstones. The streets were already dotted with green and black wheeled plastic cans rolled out for tomorrow morning's garbage pickup, and occasionally he had to sidestep around one of them. He was deep in his own thoughts, finding a curious comfort in the familiarity of the rage that was his constant companion: hating his life, feeling the entire world against him, wondering why he was even here.

He spied his homeboys a half block away, standing by a row of the cans in front of an apartment building. They were dressed like himself, in khaki pants, white pullovers and dark hoodies. They must have seen him approaching but made no sign; just continued to stand in their half-slouched cool poses, muttering to one another. Nestor, the taller and slightly older of the two, had a knit beanie and a soul patch on his chin. Rudy, clean-shaven with a full head of curly dark hair, gave an almost imperceptible nod of acknowledgment to Toby as he joined them. Mustering his own youthful cool, he extended his hand, and after a significant pause, they each gave him sideways slaps of greeting.

He knew he still wasn't completely accepted. He might have been bigger than either of them but he was younger and hadn't been on the block as long as they had. It didn't need to be articulated: they all knew he was still going to have to prove himself. That was how it worked here.

They exchanged some short, meaningless conversation before Toby pulled the backpack off his shoulder and unzipped it.

'Hey Nestor, I was thinking. You know that token you got from your uncle?'

Nestor just stared at him. His late elderly uncle had lived in New York for many years and had once given him an old city subway token. It was brass, about the size of a nickel, and it had a capital Y cut right through the metal. Nestor had put it on a gold chain and always wore it as a good luck charm, to remember his uncle. It hung from his neck now. Toby had thought it was one of the coolest things he had ever seen.

The two metal cans of spray paint briefly clunked against one another before he pulled them out of the bag. 'I had this idea.'

'What,' asked Rudy, 'you gonna paint a picture?'

'It's a Y, right? Like Yarnell. It's a perfect tag for us.'

The two looked at one another. 'Toby, ain't no *us* yet. You're not in the set, not yet, maybe not ever.'

Some set, Toby thought to himself. *Two guys. That's no gang; that's no set.* They hadn't made their mark on this street, never achieved the kind of respect a lot of guys in other neighborhoods did. Some other area gangs called them 'orphans' and other names. To be honest, they really were kinda losers. But they were all that Yarnell Street had. This was the only family available to him, and he wanted to belong, so he said nothing. If he could motivate them, he figured, they'd start to appreciate him. He was an orphan himself, or might as well be. Maybe this trio of orphans could become a family for real.

He uncapped the can of yellow and shook it so the metal ball inside rattled up and down to mix the paint within, then turned to one of the cans on the curb. He quickly sprayed three lines that converged at a hub in the center. A large bright Y.

'See? Time to make our mark on this street. Get some cred.'

Nestor and Rudy shot each other a smirk. Nestor snorted.

Toby looked back and forth at them. 'Yarnell Street, man! How 'bout some pride?'

'Hey,' said Rudy, 'wait, maybe the kid's got a point.'

'What,' said Nestor, 'you hear what he's saying, right? He's saying we got no respect here. You agree with that? You think spraying a *trademark* on junk is going to make us *respectable*, or whatever?'

Rudy nodded his head in thought for a

moment. 'Yarnell Street. Set needs a name, don' it?'

Toby started to uncap the red can to repeat the performance on another side when Nestor raised his leg and gave the can a hard kick, tipping it over onto the ground with a crash, spilling bags of garbage out onto the street. It was only a few seconds before they heard a voice from nearby yelling, 'Hey! What are you doing?'

The three turned. The light-skinned African-American guy yelling at them from the stoop wore jeans and a vinyl windbreaker. He couldn't be much older than them. He didn't look familiar. Not many guys in the neighborhood were their age, and none of them dressed that way. Looked like a school name on the jacket. There were a few college students moving into different parts of the neighborhood lately. Upscale straights.

'Leave my cans alone! Get away from there!' He took a few more steps toward them before stopping. He was a pretty good size guy, looked in good shape. Toby knew a few guys who lifted and boxed, maybe played football, and they all looked like this guy. Clearly both Rudy and Nestor were thinking twice about confronting him, despite outnumbering him three to one.

They kept their cool but Nestor simply drawled, 'The hell with 'im. Let's go.' Toby picked up his bag. They turned and sauntered away, seemingly unperturbed, never looking back, leaving the can on its side, its contents splayed out on the street. They were a half block away when the guy, who by now had righted the can and was tossing trash back into it, yelled at them, 'And leave these alone!'

Nestor uttered a few choice curses under his breath but they kept walking. Toby remained silent, secretly embarrassed that he hadn't stood up to the guy. Maybe he would have gotten knocked down, but he would have shown his homeboys something. Instead he had followed their lead and slunk away. He hoped they wouldn't see his cheeks flushing in quiet shame.

'Who the hell is that, anyway?' asked Rudy as they turned the corner at the end of Yarnell. 'Never seen him around here before.'

'I've seen him,' said Nestor, clearly still ticked off. 'Drives that burnt orange Toyota. College boy. I think he just moved in.'

Rudy jerked a thumb at Toby. 'Maybe the kid's got a point. Maybe we're not getting the respect we deserve.'

Finally Toby spoke up. 'Orange Toyota, Huh? I know the one.'

'Well, aintchoo the smart one?' Nestor spat.

'I got an idea,' Toby said. He hefted his backpack with the spray cans. 'Respect.'

This time, they were interested in what he had to say.

There wasn't much to do to occupy themselves for the next few hours, but Toby didn't feel bored. He welcomed anything that would keep him out of his apartment. They played a few games at a local pool-room. Nestor, who looked by far the oldest, bought them a six-pack of beer at a neighborhood liquor store, and they sat on a dark corner drinking and talking. Toby had laid out his plans and now they talked in greater detail about them. It was around midnight when Yarnell Street seemed sufficiently deserted for them to approach the orange Toyota without being observed. It was parked almost directly in front of the building stoop where their accuser had stood a few hours earlier, not far from the garbage cans lined up along the curb.

Toby squatted down on the curb side of the car and took out his spray cans. He began laying a huge Y across the entire side of the car in yellow, covering the passenger windows and doors. When he was done, he walked to the front of the car and sprayed a huge Y over the windshield and hood of the car. Meanwhile, Rudy had begun to knock over the garbage cans and Nestor jumped down hard on the first one, denting it heavily. He did the same on the next one. The two walked over and admired Toby's work as he repeated the process across the back of the Toyota's tailgate.

'Nice,' Nestor said, pursing his lips in a wry smile. He extended his hand, palm up. 'Way to go, big man.'

Toby slapped the palm; they locked

fingers in the next part of the handshake and then bumped fists. Rudy walked over and slapped him on the shoulder.

It was the best Toby had ever felt.

He picked up his pack and they walked away down the middle of deserted Yarnell Street, laughing quietly. There were no lights on in the windows they passed. If anybody had heard or witnessed their actions, he doubted they'd be reporting it.

His mother could blast him with all the drunken disparaging remarks she wanted. The Big Y was going to make its mark here. There would be respect. And it was because of him.

They were half a block away when they heard the footsteps behind them.

It was the guy. He was coming up very quickly on them, running like a deer. Even from down the dark street they thought they could see the fire in his eyes.

Flushed with their newfound bravado, they all turned to face him. It was three on one.

He didn't even slow down. His fist was cocked and by the time he was in swinging distance, he had unleashed a roundhouse left hand punch that caught Nestor across the side of his face, making a loud crack as it struck his cheekbone. The right fist followed closely behind, making a disturbing wet *splat* sound somewhere around his nose. Nestor fell to the ground, screeching in pain. Rudy had tried to turn to defend himself but the guy had delivered two fierce straight-finger jabs into his Adam's apple. Rudy fell to his knees, choking.

The guy turned to Toby, who had frozen. He took two steps toward him, knees slightly bent, fists clenched.

Toby had held his own in lots of fights growing up. He had to, always fighting for the respect he never seemed to get. This was just one more time. He dropped his bag and moved forward to meet the guy, looking for a vulnerable spot, but in short order, the guy had hit him square in the face three or four times, and now Toby was on his back on the cold, damp asphalt and the guy was on top of him, hitting him again and again, it seemed without end, and he was unable to do anything to stop him. Then things got muddy. Next he remembered, Nestor was shaking him and helping him sit up. The guy was gone. Blood was dripping from his nose onto his hoodie and his pullover underneath.

'Damn, what was that?' Rudy was rasping, shaking his head, rubbing his throat with one hand, still gasping for breath.

Nestor's face was already blue with bruises and smeared with blood, but he seemed more concerned about Toby, who must have looked pretty bad. 'You okay?' he asked. Toby hesitantly touched his cheek and nose and various places screamed back in pain. 'We gotta stop that bleeding. You got any rags or like that in the bag?'

Toby thought for a minute, still not very clear, and nodded. Nestor got the bag and pulled out some hunks of cloth, tore them up and started stuffing them up Toby's nose.

'We gotta get you to a doctor.'

'Not yet,' coughed Toby. 'There's something we gotta do.' He looked up at Nestor.

Nestor thought, then nodded grimly.

'You were right about this kid, Rudy. He's got the right idea. He's got heart. Come with me.'

Nestor lived by himself in a two-room walk-up on Yarnell Street. Toby and Nestor both got themselves reasonably cleaned up, but when Toby caught a look at himself in the bathroom mirror, he held his breath for a moment. His face was puffy and in various shades of red and purple. He thought his nose might be broken. Exhaustion and shock were beginning to set in, but despite having trouble thinking clearly, he knew he had to keep moving until this was done. Then he could worry about his face.

Nestor pulled out the bottom drawer of his old beat-up dresser, rummaged around behind a bunch of clothes, and pulled out a small matte black revolver. He held it up for Rudy and Toby to see. 'Ever use one of these, big man?'

Toby knew nothing about guns. He had never fired one. He had no idea what model it was, or anything about it. He shook his head, and everything north of his neck hurt.

Nestor laughed, popped and spun the cylinder. 'Time to take you to school, young man.'

It was almost sunrise when they were back at the line of mutilated cans, which had been precariously righted. The Toyota, emblazoned with the bright capital Ys, still remained at the curb. It was still that time of the early morning when late-night revelers had gone to bed and early-rising workers were not yet up. The street was still empty and silent. If the guy had called in a police report, they had probably come and gone.

'You sure this is gonna work?' asked Rudy. Nestor nodded.

'His apartment must look right out over this street. He got down here awful fast. He's angry enough, he's probably still awake. Here we go.' He kicked over one of the dented cans and leaped on top of it, this time actually breaking it with a loud *crack*.

He was right. It was only a couple of minutes before the door on the stoop opened and the guy came flying out, taking the steps two at a time.

Nestor had insisted it was going to be Toby who did it. It was, as he put it, his initiation into the family. Toby wasn't sure he could do it but, at Nestor's urging, he had stoked himself to a fury with the pain and humiliation of his wounds. The demon, anger, was always there waiting to be summoned; he let it seethe and boil up in him, fierce and frightening in its intensity. He pulled the gun out from the pocket of his hoodie, and just as he had been taught, leveled the barrel at the oncoming guy and pulled the trigger twice. The guy had brought himself up to full height, shoulders back, and presented a big target, even for a fledgling shooter. Toby caught him twice in the chest from about four feet away. The sound was surprising, just a couple of pops, but then everything went frozen and silent, like a freeze-frame in a movie: the guy in the air, his face full of surprise and anguish, and the rest of them standing there watching. And then it was as if the movie had been resumed, the air rushing back in, the roar echoing in Toby's ears, the guy falling backward onto the street.

'All right, come on, let's go,' Nestor said. They knew they couldn't press their luck. This was a neighborhood that minded its own business, up to a point, but this was something altogether different.

Rage and adrenaline still throbbed in Toby's entire body. He could hear his blood pulsing in his ears. 'Wait,' he hissed. He shoved the gun into the pocket of his sweatshirt and knelt down alongside the dead young man. He reached into his back pocket, opened up a folding knife and plunged it three times into the guy's throat. A big Y.

'What are you, crazy?' said Rudy, yanking Toby up off the body.

'Yarnell!' Toby wheezed. 'Respect!'

Nestor grabbed at Toby's shoulder. 'Damn, he's nuts, Rudy! Come on, we gotta get him outa here!'

Toby finally came out of his lunatic wrath and began to run, only a few steps behind the two older not-quite men. They tore through the streets with a speed born from a terrible moment of clarity at the full implications of what they had just done.

They finally halted near an alley, gasping for breath. 'Gimme the gun, kid,' Nestor panted. 'Come on, just give it to me!' He grabbed it out of Toby's hand and stuffed it into his pocket. 'Both of you, go home, lay low. Anybody asks, you been there all night. Got it? Now split up, take different routes back. Be cool. Go fast but don't run.'

Toby stared at Nestor as if not totally comprehending.

'Go on!' Nestor said urgently. 'Go around the block so you don't pass that guy! Take the back entrance to your building. Make sure nobody sees you. You been home sleeping, got it? Never left your apartment. You won't have a problem — your mom's been out of it all night, hasn't she?'

Toby flushed with humiliation but he simply nodded. The three resumed a brisk walk up the street. At the next corner, they headed in separate directions and were soon out of each other's sight, never to see one another in Sycamore again.

In that one evening, the Yarnell Street set had just lived its entire short life.

* ⋆ *

It took Toby a long time to calm himself sufficiently to fall asleep. He had easily snuck into his apartment in the dawning light, undetected. There hadn't been anybody on the street and his mother slept, snoring, on the couch. He examined his face in the bathroom mirror and decided it wasn't as bad as he had thought — so he'd be a little uglier from now on, big deal — but the bruises were darkening and it hurt to touch lots of places. He grabbed one of his mom's beers from the fridge and downed it, hoping it would make him sleepy and make him forget the pain, then threw himself onto his bed. Exhaustion finally won out over anxiety.

The telephone slowly brought him out of a coma-like sleep. He picked it up after about seven rings. He groggily said, ''Lo?'

'Toby, that you?'

'Nestor. What's up?'

'Listen, man, get out of there *now*. Get your stuff together and go.'

'What . . . wait. What time is it?'

141

'It's almost ten. Did you understand? Get out of there. Out of the 'hood. Out of town.'

He was still coming out of his deep sleep, trying to make sense of what he was being told. Nestor sounded different. Scared. That was it. His voice was breaking. He sounded scared.

'Toby, that guy? He was the son of a *cop!* It was on the news! They're gonna be looking for us, all of us! Go! Now!'

'Uh . . . okay.'

'You got somewhere to go, out of town? If not, just take a bus, first one you can get. And get rid of that knife, get rid of the spray paints, somewhere nobody's gonna find any of it! Hurry!'

Toby's head swirled. 'What about Rudy?'

'Rudy's not home, man! I don't know where he is! Maybe they got him already! Go on, you got no time!'

'Okay, Nestor. You too, right?'

'Damn straight. Wait, someone's at the door. That must be Rudy. Gotta run. Good luck, big man. You got heart.'

He was still dressed from the night

before. As soon as Nestor broke the connection, Toby jammed a bunch of clothes into a duffle bag and headed directly for the kitchen and the money that he knew his mother had hidden away in a cookie tin in a high cabinet. He scooped the bills out of it, shoved them in his pocket, and hurried out the back door. His mother was still sleeping off her night's drinking binge and never heard a sound. They would never see or speak to one another again and neither of them would ever care.

He had the knife and the spray cans in his bag and frantically thought about where to dispose of them. He finally settled on a large sewer opening on an empty street, big enough for him to squeeze himself partway into. He hurled everything, piece by piece, as far into the drain tunnel as he could. The sky was dark with heavy clouds, and raindrops were already falling; another big storm was coming in. With any kind of luck it would all be washed far enough away to never be found.

The station was only a short walk, and

there was a bus about to leave for Midland City. It was only as he stood at the ticket window, shrouding his bruised face with the hood of his sweatshirt, that he clandestinely inspected how much money he had grabbed from the cookie tin. He stared in astonishment at the wad of twenties. He had enough for the ticket and to tide him over for a while if he was really careful. Hopefully he'd come up with a plan before it ran out.

7

'That's not bad. Not bad at all. In fact it's amazing.'

Jilly stared at the large high-resolution monitor and its blown-up image, looking down at the dark-haired, high-cheekboned woman in the trench coat. Her hands were thrust into the pockets of her coat and her expression seemed distraught.

'That's about the best I could do,' Cam Kasten replied. 'I brought down the contrast, brought up some of the mid-tone detail, played with a few other things. I hope that helps.'

Jilly nodded, caught up in the image. 'I should say so. How accurate do you think this enhancement is?'

'Well, there's nothing that's been *added* to it. What you see is what was there . . . more or less. Sure, the software adds detail by extrapolation so in some ways it's best-guess, but it's working from the information that's inherent in the image

145

itself. I'm guessing stuff like this is open to legal challenges, but there's nothing magical about it. It's all about coaxing out details when you know how to do it.'

His explanation was getting a bit over her head despite his best efforts to stick to 'layspeak.' Jilly thought back on a prior case in which an 'enhanced' photograph had been instrumental in exonerating a convicted murderer; at the time she had been thoroughly dubious about the technology involved. She marveled at how her outlook had changed since. Even someone with a reputation for stubbornness, like herself, could come around to a new idea now and then. She shook her head and smiled. 'I suppose anything's magic when you don't know how someone does it.'

'True, that. Anyway, I put the refined image on your flash drive in a couple of common graphic formats you should be able to read no problem. I assume you want me to erase the files I've got here.'

'Yeah. What do I owe you for this?'

He raised his hands with a smile. 'Consider it a favor for someone who saved my family.'

* * *

'So how'd you grab us this room, Dan? I thought only the brass got to use this.' Leon and Dan were sitting in a newly painted conference room that featured comfortable chairs, a polished walnut table, and a large display monitor on the wall.

'The Lou said we could use it. Jilly dropped me off and she'll be back soon with the image from the traffic camera. How was your trip to Falcon Island?'

'Not very productive.' Leon gave Dan an overview of his morning with Mikal Leviev. Then he asked about their trip to Wentworth. Dan recounted Father Grabys's story of Arthur Tobias. Leon quietly listened all the way through.

'So it's true. Tobias killed Drew Vernon. Sycamore PD had the right guys.'

'Sounds like it, yeah.'

Dan could hear Leon cursing angrily under his breath.

'The priest knew all this, for what, seven, eight years? He could have cleared this up. Andy and Kelsey could have had some kind of closure. Tobias would probably

147

still be in prison.'

'He regarded it as the inviolable seal of the confession. He couldn't tell anybody. He tried to persuade Tobias to confess.'

'But he told you now. Damn.'

'So now we know. It's water under the bridge, Leon. Our focus now is, what about the other two, Rudy and Nestor? Were either of them responsible for the death of Tobias? Are they still around here somewhere?'

Leon exhaled loudly. 'Can any of that story help your own case?'

'We were particularly interested in the person that came to see Tobias. Visitor records indicated he only had one visitor in his entire eleven years there, and that was in his second year at Wentworth. He signed in as the Reverend René Montague of the World Redemption Congregation from Jacksonville, Florida.'

'Who's that?'

Dan shrugged. 'Whoever that was, Grabys believes his visit had a major effect on Tobias. I think he has some bearing on all this. We have to try to run him down.'

'From, what, nine years ago? Yeah, that

oughta be *real* easy.'

'What ought to be easy?' Jilly breezed into the room, excited. She held up the flash drive stick. 'You've got to see this.'

The file was loaded into the room's AV computer console and opened on the huge wall monitor. They stood, peering intently at the image for several minutes.

Dan finally broke the silence. 'She's got to be the one. Why else would she have been on the stairs at the time Tobias got shot?'

'But who is she?' asked Jilly. 'I'd say she's, what, in her early twenties?'

'She's Asian,' added Leon.

'I'd say Chinese,' Dan said, 'unless the imagery here is misleading.'

'Cam told me there's nothing added here. This is what he could pull from the raw image.'

'That's pretty amazing. He's got some pretty high-end equipment.'

'I already sent the original to Digital Image Forensics. They might be able to do even better. We'll need to establish an official chain of evidence through them. Maybe we can even get lucky and have facial recognition software run on her.'

'And how long is all that going to take?'

Jilly sighed. 'Forever. In the meantime we have to figure out where we can go with this.' She pointed to the screen.

'I've got a thought on that,' Leon said.

It took a few minutes to fill them in on Mary Evelyn Cho, the girlfriend of Drew Vernon. Dan immediately doubted that she could be the person in the screen shot.

'Wouldn't she be in her thirties now? This looks like a much younger woman.'

'It's not totally out of the question though, is it?' replied Leon. 'The photo's been enhanced from a night shot to begin with. The girlfriend, whatever her age, might still be young-looking. Or maybe that's someone related to her, a younger sister or whatever. The connection is worth a good look. We can't dismiss it out of hand.'

'Cho is usually a Korean name. I still think this woman looks Chinese.'

'Again, it's a rough photo. And names can change for all kinds of reasons.'

'You're right, of course, Leon,' said

Dan. 'I'm just playing devil's advocate here. How else can we follow up on this photo?'

'What if we released it to the media?' Jilly suggested. 'Maybe someone will come forward who knows her.'

'Do you think the Lou would go for that?' asked Leon.

'We'll never know until we ask.'

It turned out that Castillo was willing to allow the photo to be released to local news outlets, on the condition that Jilly or Dan would take care of the arrangements. For the next half hour there was a flurry of telephone activity as Jilly made media calls, Leon tried to track down Mary Evelyn Cho, and Dan tried to locate the mysterious Reverend Montague.

It was not difficult to locate the World Redemption Congregation's headquarters in Jacksonville, Florida. The phone was answered by a very young-sounding woman. Dan identified himself and explained he was trying to locate Reverend René Montague. The woman hesitated, then asked him to hold. It felt to Dan like he had listened through an entire recorded baroque chorale before the line was again picked up, this time by a male voice as old and creaky as an antique rocking chair.

'Detective Lee, I believe?'

'Yes, sir?'

'I'm Pastor Malcolm Farquard. I was informed you were trying to find Brother Montague?'

'That's correct, sir — I mean, Pastor.'

There was a deep sigh. 'Oh dear, I'm afraid I have unpleasant news for you. He passed away, let me see, it was over a year ago now, while on a mission overseas.'

Dan cursed under his breath, hoping the minister didn't hear him.

'Is there some way I might be of assistance to you? Were you a friend of Brother Montague?'

'No . . . no, this is in connection with an official investigation. About nine years ago, he visited someone in Wentworth Prison and was the only outside contact the convict had there. That convict became a murder victim after his recent release. I was hoping I might find out what was said between the two during that meeting. It might be important.'

'Oh dear,' Farquard repeated. 'I'm afraid I can't help you, Detective. I of course knew René quite well in his time with us. In fact it was I who welcomed him to the congregation, and baptized and ordained him, it had to be a dozen years ago now. Let me think. It wasn't unusual for any of our clergy to take a few days of personal time on occasion, but I'm sure he never mentioned any such trip to me.'

Dan was considering his next question when Farquard continued, 'But there is someone who might know something. His wife.'

'His wife?'

'Oh yes. Our clergy are allowed to marry. In fact, Sister Cilla and he accompanied one another on their missions for some years after they wed. They brought their young child with them; we allow and encourage that. They were a most wonderful pair, doing the work of the Lord with such zeal and fire. Two of the most dedicated members of our congregation.'

'Okay, then. Would it be possible to speak with Sister Cilla?'

'Unfortunately at the moment she's in . . . Mauritius, I believe. No, the Azores? I'll have to look, but she's on a mission. We have missions throughout the world, you know.'

'Is there any way I can get in touch with her? Someplace I can call?'

'I'm afraid that's difficult. If you'll leave me your phone number, I'll see what I can do.'

Dan recited his cell number and the squad room phone, having the elderly parson repeat them to be sure he got them right. Somehow he didn't hold out hope to get a return call.

'When do you expect her back in Florida, just in case I don't hear from you?'

'I can't be positive, but we rotate missions quite often. She should return in a year or so.'

When Dan hung up on the call, he had a strong feeling that was as far as it would ever go. He might find another avenue, but he suspected that the mysterious

Reverend René Montague was a dead end.

Meanwhile, Leon's first attempt to contact Mary Evelyn Cho yielded a recorded message that the telephone number was 'no longer in service.' A search for other individuals named Cho in the Denver area yielded an overwhelming list. It wasn't the first time he'd faced such a challenge, and he knew he had to work smart if he didn't want to waste a lot of time. He pulled out Roy Truax's copies of the Drew Vernon murder case file, leafed through to the interview with Mary Evelyn Cho, and lucked out. She had mentioned the names of her parents, George and Ruth Cho, in Denver. Returning to his online directories, he found no George, but there was a Ruth. Luck continued to be going his way when he dialed the number and an elderly woman picked up almost immediately. Leon identified himself and was told he had reached Ruth Cho, the mother of Mary Evelyn.

'Yes, my daughter did live in Sycamore. It was her boyfriend who was murdered all those years ago. She returned home with us and stayed in the area. She was a great help to me after my husband passed away.'

'I'm sorry for your loss, ma'am.'

'Well, the accident was four years ago now. We finally reached the point where we both could move on and I was able to tell Mary Evelyn she didn't need to be close to me anymore. She's still a young woman and needs to live her own life.'

'So she moved recently, I gather?'

'Oh, yes. She found a new job. She's been going back and forth between here and there for several weeks now, arranging the move. She'll be settling into her new apartment tonight, in fact.'

'Excuse me, ma'am, you said 'there.' Where exactly is 'there'?'

'Why, *there*! I meant that literally! Where you are! She's returned to your area.'

'So I should be able to reach her at her new place tomorrow morning?'

'I would think so. Her flight gets in fairly late tonight. Would you like me to call and have her contact you?'

'That won't be necessary, thank you.

Actually, I'd prefer to go by in person to talk to her. Could I get her new address?'

She gave Leon an address. The street was familiar.

'A couple of final questions, Mrs. Cho. Did your daughter ever marry?'

'Oh, no. She's always remained single.'

'Are there any younger members of your immediate family, any grandchildren, nieces or nephews or such?'

'No, I'm afraid not.' She sighed heavily. The silence hung over the phone awkwardly. Then she began to talk . . . about her early life, random things. He knew he had to get off the phone, but having elderly relatives who lived in their own solitude, he understood. He respectfully let her reminisce about her family for a few minutes before finding an opportune moment to take his leave.

Leon knew the street she had given him, Kensington Court. It was half a mile from the Pomeroy Tunnel. He thanked Mrs. Cho and hung up, feeling his anticipation rising.

Art Dowdy was at his desk, squinting at the monitor of his computer, by the time that Leon was able to join him.

'Sorry, Art. We had a lot of catching up on the Tobias case.'

'How's that going?'

'I might have just lucked into something. We'll see. Any word on our floater?'

'SID got lucky and got an ID off the prints. I was able to track down some more on him. Here's the info.'

Leon bent over to look at the screen over his partner's shoulder and read the name off the file.

'He's an ex-con, on parole. He was staying at a halfway house. Maybe we can get a lead there . . . '

'Damn,' muttered Leon. 'Hold on!' He frantically looked around the squad room to see if Jilly or Dan were still to be found.

★   ★   ★

'I can't believe this! What's going on with my house, anyway? Nobody's ever gonna want to place someone here after this! They might even shut me down completely!'

He was probably right, and that would be all for the better.

Arlo Merchant was sitting at the familiar kitchen table, cradling his head in his hands, bemoaning his fate to nobody in particular. Les Lonergan sat next to him, looking bewildered and uncomfortable.

Jilly was back in the exact same seat she had taken a few days earlier. This time the detective sitting next to her was Leon.

Merchant suddenly ceased his lamentations. He looked up as if remembering what was going on. 'Has anybody notified his parole officer?'

'My partner's talking with him right now,' Leon said.

'What was the last time you saw Sammy?' Jilly asked.

'It's been a while. I think he was working a lot.'

'What was the last time he signed in?'

Merchant shook his head. 'I don't know. I didn't see him all day yesterday, which was Thursday.'

'And you haven't checked the sign-in sheets, have you?'

'Look, do you realize how much there

159

is to do around here? There's just me. I have to do everything. Sometimes stuff gets by me. This is crazy, just crazy! What happened to him?'

'That's what we want to know.' Leon stared at Lonergan as he spoke.

'What?' Lonergan piped up. '*I* don't know what happened to him!'

'Why didn't you tell us the other day about what you saw?' Jilly asked. 'Sammy said he hadn't spoken with Arthur Tobias since he had arrived. You knew that was a lie. You saw Tobias leave Sunday night and you saw Sammy walk out after him. You never spoke up. For all you know, Sammy might still be alive if you'd said something.'

'What, you think he got killed because of Tobias? How could I have known that? I couldn't say anything and put him on the spot like that. I'm still trying to do my own time here. I figured whatever Sammy had going on was his concern, not mine.'

'You guys don't think Sammy killed Tobias, do you?' Merchant asked, eyes wide as if he still couldn't believe what was happening.

'He might have fingered him for someone else,' said Leon, 'and that might be what got him killed as well. So the question is, who's come around here looking for Sammy since Tobias arrived?'

'Nobody,' said Merchant. 'Visitors have to sign in. Nobody ever signed in to visit Sammy.'

Jilly and Leon exchanged a look, both straining to avoid dubious expressions, then looked at Lonergan.

'What?' he said plaintively.

Likable Leon had the ability to become Scary Leon on the turn of a dime. He focused an intense glare on the ex-con. 'Les, you could be on the hook for withholding evidence. That's enough to revoke your parole and send you back to Wentworth, maybe for a long time. If you can do anything in your own defense, now's the time to start doing it.'

Les sighed. 'Come to think of it, there was this odd guy hanging around out front on Saturday . . . '

8

Dan was greeted on arrival at work Friday morning by the flashing of his desk phone.

'Detective Lee speaking.'

'Detective Lee, this is Cilla Montague. I was told you were trying to reach me.'

Dan dropped himself into his chair. 'Thank you for calling me . . . is it Reverend Montague?'

'They call me Sister Montague in the congregation. Just plain Cilla is fine.'

'I have to say, the connection's good. I expected we might have trouble talking. And I'm not sure what time it is where you are . . . '

'What do you mean? I'm in Florida. I believe we're three hours later than you, is that right? It's not quite eleven.'

'I thought you were in the Azores. Pastor Farquard said — '

She laughed. 'The Azores . . . ? Oh, the pastor is a dear, dear man. He means so

162

much to all of us. But I'm afraid he's a bit absent-minded of late. No, I've been back in the United States for a number of months now.' Her voice grew more serious. 'I think I know what your call was about. It's René.'

'Yes, that's right.'

'He knew this day might come. He told me all about it and prepared me for it.' She took a deep breath. 'The man called Toby, he's dead, isn't he?'

That took Dan aback for a moment. 'That's right. You knew about him?'

'He was the last of them. They're all gone now.' Another long pause. 'I think you know who my husband really was.'

'I had a hunch. He turned up in Florida at the congregation somewhere around twelve years ago. He was either Rudy Serazin or Nestor Lowell, wasn't he?'

'He was Rudy Serazin. That was another lifetime ago for him. How much of the story do you know, Detective?'

'I know about the Yarnell Street boys. There were three of them. They were suspected of killing a young man named

163

Drew Vernon in the city of Sycamore about fourteen years ago. They all vanished. Only Andrew Tobias, the man you called Toby, ever turned up again, when he was arrested and sent to Wentworth Prison.'

'René told me the entire story. I think I'm the only one to whom he ever entrusted it. You have to understand, when he came into the church, the pastor told him his past meant nothing. The congregation's mission has always been redemption. He accepted him, baptized him, and urged him to put his old life behind and begin a new one. And so he did. But it was important to René to tell *someone* about it.'

'Wait. You said they're all gone now. Nestor Lowell is also dead?'

'He was killed almost immediately after the incident. René — well, he was still Rudy — heard it happen.'

'What?'

'Only a few hours after the boy had been killed, Rudy heard the news that he was the son of a policeman. He knew what that meant. They would have to get away immediately. Nestor was more or less their leader, so Rudy decided to go to Nestor's to make sure he knew and get his advice. When he got to the apartment door, he saw it was partway open. He heard voices and then muffled shots, like a gun covered by a pillow or something. He ran back down the stairs and out onto the street. It was shortly after that he was apprehended by the police, still disoriented.'

Dan struggled to wrap his head around what he had just heard. 'So who killed Nestor?'

"René first thought that it was Toby. He and Nestor were a bit scared of him; they called him a loose cannon, troubled and unpredictable. Once Toby had actually killed someone, who knows what had been unleashed. It was only later that René began to wonder, what if, rather than Toby, someone else was coming after all of them? Either way, he was terrified that he'd be next.

'He kept quiet and pretty soon the police had to release him. There was no murder weapon, no evidence. He hadn't done the shooting so there was no gunshot residue on him. He only had an insubstantial bruise on his throat; any blood on the victim from the fight would have come from Toby or Nestor. They had nothing, no reason to detain him any longer. But he was convinced he was in danger and might only have a small window of opportunity, so he immediately left town. He found his way across the country to Florida, adopted a new identity, and not long after that encountered Pastor Farquard.'

'He became Brother René Montague.'

'That's right. But something else happened, Detective. The whole experience had terrified him with the dark potential of the soul. He was wracked with guilt. I'm convinced he was a good man from the beginning, but adrift, without a role model or a guiding moral light. As he became more spiritually aware, he desperately sought redemption for his part in that horrible crime.'

'Whether or not he pulled the trigger,' said Dan, 'he was at least an accomplice to first-degree murder. He wasn't blameless. The case was never closed; no arrests, no convictions. Justice was not done. He should have gone back, turned himself in.'

'Believe me, he understood that. The pastor was willing to let him clean the slate, but Rene knew the day would come when he would have to step forward to the authorities.'

'So why didn't he?'

'He was frightened. You've heard the expression 'looking over one's shoulder'? That was, sometimes literally, Rene. Many times he told me he thought himself a coward and prayed for the courage and strength to do the right thing. But the fact that Nestor had been killed so quickly and efficiently weighed on him. He was sure that would happen to him the moment he surfaced, whether it was Toby or someone else who would be coming; and not only after him, but also after me and our son.'

'He learned that Toby was at Wentworth.'

'Yes. Over the years, he continually checked for any news of him. He risked a trip across the country to visit him, and to reveal who he really was. Redemption is our major tenet, and René felt a responsibility for his friend's salvation. Toby killed the young man in Sycamore, and maybe he'd killed Nestor. He'd been a ferociously angry young man from the outset; he'd pulled the trigger on at least one person, and it had changed his life.'

'That was a brave thing for René to have done, to seek him out and face him.'

'He knew he had to do it for his own soul, Detective. They were able to talk frankly and sincerely. He said Toby broke down in tears at one point. René departed that day convinced of two things: Toby was not Nestor's killer, and he regretted having killed Drew Vernon. René was still worried that someone was looking for them both, but there was also was a huge sense of relief. Can you understand that?'

'I think so. By the way, according to the prison chaplain, whatever was said at that meeting, Rene's visit had a profound effect on Toby from that moment on. It did change him.'

'René would have been happy. He hoped he'd made some small difference.

Toby was not a religious man by any means. It was clear he wasn't going to embrace any kind of faith, but René hoped at least he could make him start to think.'

'For what it's worth, Toby did a *lot* of thinking over the next nine years. It would seem he wanted to find his own redemption, in his own way, for his past.'

Cilla Montague sighed. 'And his past finally caught up with him. So now they're all gone, all three of them.'

'If I might ask, Sister Cilla, how did your husband die?'

'It was during a hurricane in the Caribbean. We were on a small island. He drowned saving the lives of several small children, including our own son. I hope he felt he'd finally settled his debt.'

'There are those who don't believe it works that way,' said Dan somberly, 'that it's not a profit-loss statement. You can't tally a life or lives against one another . . . neither René nor whoever killed Nestor and Toby.'

'I get your point. All lives are sacred. But the defining tenet of our congregation, Detective, is that redemption is always possible and you can always be forgiven as long as you don't despair . . . '

Dan wasn't sure he could accept that, and in fact doubted it deeply . . . but he hoped she was right.

They spoke for a few more minutes before the line grew quiet. Dan thanked Sister Cilla for her call and offered his condolences. After he had hung up, he sat at his desk for a long time, lost in thought.

What a remarkable account. Two wanted men who hid in plain sight, and possibly an avenger who bided their time patiently over years, waiting for them to re-surface?

Or . . . passed the mission on to another generation?

He thought about the young Asian woman on the Pomeroy stairs.

He hadn't realized that Jilly was standing in front of his desk until she cleared her throat and interrupted his brooding. He snapped back to reality.

'Morning, Dan. What's up? Looks serious.'

'I'm thinking maybe Leon might be on

to something after all.'

He told her the whole story. Jilly nodded. She hadn't had the chance to fill Dan in on the previous day's interview at Merchant's boarding house and her subsequent conversation with Leon, so now she did so. When she was finished, Dan shook his head.

'So this Mary Evelyn Cho is here in town?'

'Leon is probably talking to her right about now, if she's where her mother said she'd be.'

'Maybe she's the key to it all. And if so, how does this whole thing with Sammy's murder fit in?'

'It's hard for me to believe that it's unrelated. Les couldn't give us much of a description of the guy he saw with Sammy. He just said he was a middle-aged guy in a dark-colored windbreaker and a flat cap who stood in the shadows of the trees. He couldn't even tell us if the guy was light — or dark-skinned.'

'Our friend Les isn't exactly rocket-scientist material, is he?'

'You really are getting more sarcastic

with time, you know that? Anyway, we're going to have to keep unraveling all the players here. If Mary Evelyn is connected, it doesn't seem like she'd fit the profile of our mysterious lady on camera.'

Dan pursed his lips. 'If not her, maybe there's still another, younger person connected with her somehow. It just keeps getting more complicated. Let's hope Leon comes up with some answers with Mary Evelyn.'

★   ★   ★

At that very moment, Leon was standing in front of the apartment house at 2257 Kensington Court. It was a tidy two-block-long street of older well-preserved buildings, nicely shaded by mature ash trees. 2257 was a brick and stone edifice that had been renovated to add handi-capped access ramps up to new wide glass entrance doors. He strolled up one of the ramps rather than take the wide stone steps. The front door was locked and required a tenant to be buzzed to allow access. A slab of cardboard had already been inserted into number 112 that read CHO in large block letters. He pressed the corresponding button and the intercom crackled to life.

'Yes, may I help you?'

'I'm Police Detective Leon Simpkins. I'm looking for Mary Evelyn Cho?'

'That would be me. I'll come to the front door and you can show me your credentials and then I'll let you in.'

Leon pulled out his identity card and badge and waited, wondering why it was taking her so long. If the numbering of her apartment ran true to form, she was right there on the first floor. Through the glass doors, he could see the long carpeted hall that went past the vestibule with its benches, mailboxes and elevators. She finally did show up coming down the corridor, and at the door she inspected Leon's ID carefully before opening the door to admit him. She was a serious-looking woman, clearly in her thirties, with short frosted hair and fashionably heavy black glasses.

Leon now understood that she really hadn't taken all that much time to get from her apartment to the front door, considering she was in a wheelchair.

★ ★ ★

'You'll have to forgive me. I just arrived last night and I'm still in the process of setting up the place,' she said as she skillfully wheeled around her spacious kitchen to her refrigerator. 'Can I get you some milk for that coffee?'

'No, black is fine, thank you.'

She effortlessly spun her chair around and returned to the kitchen table, parking her chair across from him. 'This is a great building. When the new owners took it over, they redesigned it with people like myself in mind. It's so easy to get around.'

'You seem to be doing all right,' Leon observed.

'It's been a few years now since the accident,' Mary Evelyn replied sunnily. 'I guess I'm a quick study. I've gotten used to navigating around. I can even drive.'

'I'm sorry . . . the accident?'

'Oh, I thought my mom had told you.

174

The car accident, the one that killed my dad.'

Leon hesitated. 'Your mom told you I called?'

'Oh sure. She called me last night, soon as I was off the plane.'

'You know, she talked about a lot of things, and she mentioned your father had passed, but she never told me about . . . well, about the rest.'

'About me being in this chair, you mean. That sounds like my mom. I bet she told you about her family coming over from Korea and so forth.'

'As a matter of fact, she did talk a little about that.'

'More than a little, if I guess right. Mom can be a chatterbox. But she didn't tell you I can't walk, huh? Or even that I'd been in the accident? It figures. She's kinda guilt-ridden. She insisted on driving that night. We got hit by a drunk driver and she came out okay, and it's haunted her ever since. It's one of the reasons I stayed with her the last few years. But she's a truly amazing woman. She gradually started to become healthier and more functional again until I felt it was safe to leave her. She even insisted it was time for me to move on and start looking after myself again.'

'I'm surprised you'd come back here, so close to Sycamore. There couldn't be very good memories.'

'You mean Drew. I don't think I could have come back here ten years ago. That was pretty traumatic, you're right. I had to think long and hard when I got a great job offer here. My mom encouraged me to do it.'

'What kind of job?'

'At Newland Medical Center, maybe a half mile from here. I'm a mental health counselor. Talk about ironies: my specialty is grief counseling. I originally went into it, I think, to deal with my own issues . . . and that was even before Spencer.'

'Excuse me, Spencer?'

'He was sort of my boyfriend a few years after I moved to Denver. He worked in the same psychological service center I did. The relationship wasn't as serious as it had been with Drew, but we were close enough that it hit me hard when he

176

keeled over while we were having dinner in a restaurant one night. He had an aneurism. He didn't make it through the next morning.'

'My God, I'm so sorry.'

Mary Evelyn shrugged. 'I decided to work through it, to apply what I was learning in my grief counseling experiences.'

'Has it worked?'

Her smile was tinged with sadness. 'Yeah. It helped a lot. You know, there was one morning I woke up, just before the accident, and I realized it had been weeks since I even thought about Drew or about Spencer. I forced myself to think about each of them, to try to visualize each of them, and they were fading. I mean, they'll both always be there inside me, you know? But the images didn't hurt very much anymore. I've heard that sooner or later our minds of necessity remove the pain and keep the happy memories, out of self-preservation. Do you believe that, Detective?'

'I'm afraid I know that's not always true. I've seen too many times, I'm afraid, where the pain stayed fresh no matter how long.'

She nodded. 'Yes, I suppose I have too. But I've also helped many of the bereaved to heal, so maybe it's the luck of the draw.' She stared at Leon with that same sad smile. 'That did kind of kill my appetite for relationships, though, at least up until now. But I'm okay with that. I devoted myself to helping my mom heal, and to my job helping others, and now maybe I can make a new life for myself here, try to meet someone and start over.' She looked down at her wheelchair. 'You know, it's funny. Somehow I think my grief was a bigger impediment to starting over than not having the use of my legs. I don't think of myself as all that different from anyone else.'

Leon, feeling a bit uncomfortable, diverted the subject back. 'They never found Drew's killers.'

She nodded. 'I figured that. I haven't heard anything about the case in many years, but I always assumed I'd be contacted if they did find someone. Frankly, I doubt they ever will. I've seen a lot of senseless urban violence in my work. I gave up on finding closure way back when.'

Leon eyed her guardedly. 'One of the suspected killers turned up recently.'

'Really? Is he in custody? Where did they find him?'

'He's dead. He died not far from here, in fact.'

'You mean he was around here all this time? What happened?'

Leon told her the bare bones of the story, keeping a lookout for any kind of tell: an involuntary reaction, a reference to some detail he hadn't divulged. If she was putting on a show, she was good indeed. But as they continued to talk, the nagging feeling grew ever stronger in him that this was not someone who had been involved in the murder he was investigating. By the time he thanked her and left, he harbored powerful doubts she could be the one.

So where did that leave them now? A young Asian woman and a nondescript middle-aged guy with no apparent connection to anything or anybody else. He paced off his irritability up and down the block before returning to his car. His mobile phone started ringing just before he had reached the vehicle.

'Leon, it's Jilly. How's it going?'

'Worse before it gets better, I'm afraid.'

'Can you get back here? You'll want to be here for this. Someone is coming in.'

'And who's that?'

'She saw the photo on the news. She says it's her niece. She's bringing her in now.'

9

Leon looked at the monitor, angling down on the two apprehensive-looking women sitting in the interview room.

'They're already scared,' he said quietly. 'I'm thinking three of us all trooping in there is going to seem pretty intimidating to them, especially if one is a big guy in a bad mood. You two go in. I'll watch and listen from out here.'

Jilly and Dan entered and introduced themselves in English. Neither of the women rose. The older woman, who looked to be perhaps in her forties, said she was Eline Fong and introduced her niece, Xi Lin, who shyly smiled at them.

'I'm sorry, my niece does not speak much English,' Fong said quietly. 'I'll translate for her.'

Xi Lin certainly looked to be the young woman in the video image. She was shy and attractive, with long dark hair. She sat nervously, looking back and forth at the detectives as they sat down across from the two women.

'Thank you for coming in,' Jilly began.

'I saw Xi Lin's picture on the news today and knew we had to come. I can explain why she was there that night.'

'Well, then. Please.'

'My niece has only recently arrived here from a small village in Talshan, in China. My sister and brother-in-law thought she would have a better future if she came here, where she can study and find better opportunities. I own a restaurant, the Fortune Inn, which is near the university. I offered to employ her and give her a home while she acclimated to this country.'

Xi Lin spoke hurriedly to Eline Fong and the two conversed animatedly in their native language for some time. Dan took careful interest.

'She does not feel all that comfortable here yet. We hope she'll improve her English as she meets customers, but as you probably know, there are many Chinese students here, and one reason our restaurant does so well is that it is popular with them. Unfortunately they are often quite happy to converse with her in Cantonese rather than English. As a result, her ability to communicate in English is not developing as quickly as I had hoped.'

Xi Lin, seemingly concerned about making a point, again spoke rapidly to her aunt, who replied abruptly, cutting her off.

'So please tell us,' Jilly said, looking back and forth between them, 'just how she found herself on those steps so late at night?'

'My niece likes to go out with the students after work. I discourage her from this because I worry about her, and this illustrates exactly why, but she disregarded me. They stayed out late and when the group broke up, she found herself separated from them and lost. She wandered around, trying to find her way back home. Finally she found familiar landmarks and returned, but I was terribly worried.' Her voice turned stern. 'I waited up for her and scolded her. I hope it taught her a lesson.'

Again Xi Lin spoke urgently to her aunt, who waved at her as if to dismiss her. That was when Dan jumped in, speaking in fluent Cantonese to the young woman. It took everyone else at the table by surprise. Xi Lin began to reply but Eline Fong interrupted her to speak to Dan.

'Please,' Dan said politely in English to the older woman, 'I'd like Xi Lin to answer my questions herself.'

The aunt looked none too happy but complied, sitting back with arms folded as Xi Lin and Dan carried on a back-and-forth. Finally Dan smiled at the young woman and nodded.

'She saw what happened,' Dan said to Jilly. 'Tobias was there. But somebody else had arrived before him who was lying in wait. She saw that person kill him.'

Dan spoke further with Xi Lin, trying to sound reassuring. The girl looked vulnerable and terrified, but Jilly could see that Dan was gently coaxing more information out of her.

'She was walking around the traffic circle, not certain of her surroundings, but it was well lit so she felt safe. She had a new phone but didn't yet have her aunt's number or anyone else's. She noticed the stairs and thought that Pomeroy Avenue at the foot of them looked vaguely familiar, so she started down the stairs. She says that when she got to the midway landing, there was a man coming up the stairs from below and he frightened her. He had a mean scowl on his face. She turned from him and got out her phone and tried to call 911, hoping perhaps someone on the line would be able to speak her language. Then she saw the other man, coming down the stairs from above towards her.'

'Tobias,' said Jilly.

'Yes. At first she was just as scared of him as of the other man, since he was very big and disfigured, but something made her decide that he was safer than the other, maybe would even protect her from the other man. She says he smiled at her and just looked kind. She thought he asked if he could help, and she started to hand him her phone, but suddenly the other man stepped out of the shadows past her, raised a pistol, and shot him.

She doesn't remember much except she ran down the stairs and across Pomeroy as fast as she could. She says she does remember almost getting hit by a car that blared its horn at her.'

'Why didn't she come forward and report any of this before now?'

Dan shot a sideways glance at Eline Fong, clearly intended only for Jilly to see. 'She was afraid because she thought she'd get in trouble and be sent back to China.'

'I knew nothing of any of this until today, when she told me!' Eline Fong declared. 'What a terrible thing!'

Jilly turned to her. 'Ms. Fong, you and your niece need not worry. Xi Lin is in no trouble. You both have done the right thing to come to us today.' She turned to Xi Lin, who stared back at her with wide troubled eyes. 'What we need to know now is if she saw anything that might help us identify the man who did the shooting.'

Dan spoke to them in Cantonese; Jilly assumed he was repeating what she had said. Neither seemed to want to answer.

'It might not be necessary for her to

testify in open court. We'll try to protect her.' Dan again translated. Finally the young woman nodded her head, hesitantly at first and then more vigorously. She spoke rapidly to Dan, who nodded and made a few notes on his pad.

A thought seemed to come to Dan and he spoke further with the two women. Fong seemed a bit hesitant at something that had been said but finally nodded to Dan, clearly with some reservation. Xi Lin also nodded in agreement, somewhat more willingly, to whatever had been said.

'I've asked Xi Lin if she wouldn't mind looking at some photos of possible suspects,' Dan said to Jilly. 'And I've explained to Ms. Fong that we prefer to have the witness do this by herself, so she's agreed to wait outside.' The older woman rose from her seat along with the detectives.

Outside the room, Dan directed Ms. Fong to a seat in the hallway and said he'd be right back with a set of photos. Jilly, understanding something was up, followed him around the corner of the corridor.

'I'll put a six-pack of random photos together for her. Can you babysit the aunt for a few minutes? I really just want to speak with the niece alone for a minute.'

'What's up, Dan?'

'There's something going on here. I think I know what it is. Xi Lin's family sent her here because they hoped she'd have better opportunities. That's not unusual in a rural village when there's a relative who's established themselves in a city in the United States. But often it doesn't work out the way they hoped. The American relative sees an opportunity to utilize them as cheap labor. They isolate them and keep them focused on work. I think that the aunt knows more than she's letting on. Xi Lin is afraid to say anything in her presence that might be embarrassing to her.'

'Okay, Dan. Go for it.'

As Dan hustled off to assemble a set of photos, Jilly returned to sit with Eline Fong, joined shortly by Leon. He had mellowed sufficiently to give his best Likable Leon smile to the restaurateur, inspiring a hesitant smile in return.

The dialogue did not take very long and soon Dan and Xi Lin emerged from the interview room, chatting amiably. Dan thanked both women in Cantonese and farewells were exchanged. Dan and Jilly waited, smiles hanging suspended, until Leon had escorted the women to the elevator.

'Okay, Dan. So?'

'It's pretty much as I suspected. The aunt's working her long hours seven days a week and not letting her get out to do much. She told us she's encouraging Xi Lin to learn English but actually in her concern about losing her, she's effectively preventing that. The restaurant closes early on Sunday. Xi Lin had snuck out with a boyfriend, it would seem.'

'A boyfriend?'

'Well, a potential boyfriend. Apparently things didn't go well on the date and they argued over something. He sounds like a real jerk, just let her walk off at the movie. Anyway, she had no idea where she was and just stared wandering. She was pretty far away from the restaurant and this is a big city.'

'She had a phone.'

'Yeah. And I'm sure she did have her aunt's phone number at the restaurant, but she wasn't about to call her. That girl may not look it, but she's very self-possessed. Her aunt would call her rebellious. She had the guts to go off on a date and to leave the guy behind. She was sure she'd find her way home . . . and she did, after her misadventure.'

Jilly nodded. 'A different story than we first heard. She couldn't contradict the aunt or speak freely in her presence. I'm surprised she trusted you.'

'It was a calculated gamble. I'm sure she's highly suspicious of authority figures in general, given her background . . . and things haven't improved in that area since she arrived here.'

'I guess you just inspire trust. Or she found you handsome.'

Dan actually flushed. 'It didn't hurt that my own family comes from an area near Talshan. I just lucked out. I also made up a few things about my own rebelliousness with my family. I said my situation was similar to hers. We got conspiratorial, you know?'

'Yeah. I can't imagine you were ever actually rebellious.'

'Hey, maybe I'm not as straight an arrow as you guys all think.'

'Uh huh. Anyway, is this going anywhere?'

'Besides the fact her story now makes more sense? Probably not. I feel bad for her but I don't think there's anything that can be done. She's got a real spirit. I think she'll be solving her own problem ultimately.'

'So what about her ID of the shooter, any luck?'

'Well, of course, she didn't ID any of the photos I put together. And it was dark, and she was scared. She wasn't sure of the guy's race or color but she did give me a surprisingly good description of his approximate height and weight, what he was wearing, his mustache, and his eyes.'

'His eyes?'

'Yeah. Even in the dark, she said his eyes were burning, that was the word she used. He apparently stared right at her. She said his expression was like death.

She was sure he was going to kill her too. But he just let her run away.'

Leon had returned to the conversation in time to hear Dan's last comment. 'What did she say the guy looked like?'

As Dan repeated Xi Lin's description as closely as he could, Leon began to scowl.

'And what was he wearing?'

'A dark overcoat, she was pretty sure it was dark green, and one of those tweedy flat caps.'

'Any chance this could be one of the guys who was in the bar, who maybe doubled back to follow Tobias?'

'Certainly possible.'

'I'm thinking you might want to head back to that bar and see if one of those guys was dressed like that or meets the description.'

'Good idea.'

'And if you don't mind, I'd like to join you.'

⋆　⋆　⋆

Lannie O'Casey was still behind the bar and his best customer, Wanda, was still at the side table. Dan introduced Leon and asked the owner if he'd take a moment and come sit with them. It was still early and the Friday night crowd hadn't started trickling in yet, so he joined them.

'This is about last Sunday, I presume,' O'Casey said as he sat down.

'How much do you remember about the other guys who were here that night?' Dan asked.

'Not sure. They were just two guys, never saw either of them before.'

'Did they come in together?'

'No, I don't think so. They were both just sitting at the bar and the one guy walked over to the dart board and asked the other fellow if he played. Next thing you knew, they were deep into a match.'

'Do you remember what either of them might have been wearing?'

O'Casey thought and shook his head. 'Hard to say now.'

Wanda piped up from the next table. 'The shorter fellow, the darker one, he had a grey sweatshirt and jeans. The taller one, he was a little older and a little lighter, he had a dark shirt and pants and wore one of those newsboy caps.'

They all turned to look at Wanda. 'Newsboy cap,' Leon repeated. 'Like a flat cap?'

'Yes, dearie. It was kind of grey or beige wool.'

'Did this guy have a coat or a jacket?'

'Now that I think of it, yes. Both of them had slung their coats over the backs of chairs. He had a long, sort of greenish coat.'

'You've got a good memory,' Dan said. Wanda smiled.

'Nothing here gets past her,' O'Casey laughed. 'She's the official historian of the Albatross, that one.'

'Can you remember anything else about this man?' Leon continued. 'Any facial hair, anything like that?'

'I remember he had a grey mustache. A rather short but bushy one.' She ran a finger over her upper lip. 'And I remember he must have been a very good dart player, because the other man kept complaining how he kept beating him.'

'Would you mind joining us at the table here in a minute, ma'am?' Leon asked, reaching into the pocket of his sport coat. 'I'd like to show each of you, one at a time, a set of photos. Let us know if any of them looks at all familiar.'

Dan raised his eyebrows. He hadn't expected Leon to have photographs, but by this point he understood. There was only one place this was all going to end.

10

They were back on Andy's porch in Altuve, but this time there were no beers and no small talk. Leon had shown up unannounced early Saturday morning. When Kelsey answered the door, he had simply said hello and asked if Andy would come out. They now sat glumly in the same chairs as before, looking out at the same beach a block away.

'Two visits in a week, Leon. Gotta be a record.'

'Surprised you're not out on the *Flatfoot*.'

'Thinking about it. Maybe tomorrow. That's a nice thing about retirement, you can make last-minute decisions.'

'Speaking of the *Flatfoot*, there's a funny thing about that boat.'

'And what would that be?'

'There's a little marina up the coast that has a record of the *Flatfoot* being harbored there last weekend.'

'That so? And how would you have found out something like that, and why?'

'Andy, I'm a detective. There's a whole bunch of us in Personal Crimes to follow up on stuff like that. Remember?'

Andy sighed and just stared ahead, not looking over at Leon.

'You didn't catch no bluefin. Where'd you find that fish for Kelsey to clean, some fish market somewhere?'

The silence got thick. There was just the rolling surf off in the distance on the overcast beach, and Leon directing a steely gaze at Andy, and Andy staring straight ahead, both men stock still.

'Andy, I know what happened. I'm missing a few small things, but I know enough.'

Andy cursed under his breath, a short string of sibilant profanities. 'It was that damned girl, wasn't it?'

Leon said nothing. Andy still would not look at him.

'For the life of me, I got *no* idea what she was doing there. Two in the damned morning, for God's sake!'

'What were *you* doing there?'

Andy finally turned and glowered back at Leon. 'What the hell do you think I was doing there?'

'So you, what, followed him from the bar? Did Sammy Figueroa tell you where you'd find him?'

'Sammy. So he turned up.'

'They pulled him out of the harbor the other day. Art and I actually caught the case.'

'Damnation, when the luck goes bad, it goes bad.'

'Walk me back a little bit here. How did you know Figueroa?'

'I didn't. All I knew was he lived in that halfwit's halfway house. I reached out to him, as we say.'

'So he was supposed to call you when opportunity struck and you might catch Tobias somewhere?'

'The guy needed dough, like all losers. Said something about wanting to go to school or something. Whatever. Like I cared. He jumped at the chance to simply provide me some intel; just make a phone call, that was it. I gave him the number of a burner I picked up.'

'But then he found out Tobias got killed. That wasn't what he'd signed up for.'

Andy sighed and rubbed the morning stubble on his chin. 'After Garvey and Lee came around and talked to him, he called me back in a panic, said I had gotten him in way deeper than he expected. He had to get out of town fast, jump parole, and he needed a *lot* more money from me to not say anything.'

'He said all this over the phone, did he?'

'Yep. What he wanted was a lot more than I had on hand. I could've put it together, but you and I both know that wouldn't have been the end of it, not by a long shot. So I told him I'd drive up late Tuesday, meet him out at the end of the pier and bring the money. My real plan was to see if I could calm him down and talk some sense into him.'

'Clearly that didn't happen.'

'No.' Andy sighed deeply. 'No, it didn't. Crazy loudmouthed knucklehead. Clearly a loose cannon.'

'Security risk for sure. I'm kinda

surprised at you, Andy. Pretty sloppy, shooting him and just dropping him in the water. Are we going to find it's the same .38 as Tobias, by the way?'

'If SID does its job, yeah. And it *was* sloppy. It all just sorta happened. We were out at the end of the pier. It's long; you know how far out into the bay it goes. I shot him, he staggered away and fell in. I wish I'd had him out on the boat. Maybe I could have scared him more effectively. But there was no way I was bringing him down here, showing him where I lived. The whole thing was just, whattaya call it, impromptu.'

'But he'd hooked you up with Tobias.'

'He followed him to that bar and called me. I was hanging out in town waiting for his call so I got myself over there pretty quick. I wasn't quite sure how I was going to play it; I figured I'd improvise.'

'You would've made a good undercover guy. He never made you. You were just one of the 'gentlemen of color' in the Albatross playing darts, am I right?'

'Uh huh. Where'd you get that from?'

'Lady at the bar called you that.'

'The old barfly. Well, I don't get called a gentleman of any kind all that often, so I'll let it pass. Anyway, I couldn't involve Tobias in a conversation so I waited him out. I knew where he'd be going at closing time. I figured it was perfect. I was parked right around the corner, and as soon as I was out of his sight, I lit out for the car and drove like a demon to get to the bottom of the stairs. I was just coming up to the landing when I saw this shadow up there. It was that crazy girl. She saw me and started to freak out. She had her phone out and she was frantically dialing and yelling into it in, like, Chinese or something. Then she looked up the stairs and froze. I knew who that had to be.'

'So you plugged Tobias on the dark landing.'

'*Plugged*'? Been reading detective novels, Leon? She actually helped me, unwittingly. She handed him her phone, for God's sake. He was momentarily distracted. I just walked up and . . . that was it.'

'She ran down the stairs. You didn't try to take out the witness?'

'I let her run. I couldn't kill an innocent.'

Leon let that irony pass.

'Then you took the time to carve that Y in his throat. What was that all about?'

'Last-minute inspiration. If the Yarnell Street story came out, it would look like one of his old compadres had come back and iced him.'

'Weren't you worried that the lady would call the police?'

'I figured out she couldn't speak English. She could hardly dial 911, for God's sake. Whatever she was doing out there in the middle of the night, I figured she wasn't in a hurry to get herself involved in anything. And it seems I was right, at least for a while.'

'But she got caught on a traffic cam. How did you get out of there without being seen?'

'A traffic cam.' Andy shook his head. 'So there was one down there. I wasn't sure. There's usually a blasted camera somewhere. But I made sure there was nobody driving by — at that time of night, it wasn't hard — and I bent down low coming down the steps, stayed close to the wall when I got to the sidewalk, and snuck back to my car like a damned spy.'

'Were you hoping the Y mark on Tobias would rouse Rudy Serazin, and maybe he'd come back to find out what happened?'

'I mainly considered that it would deflect suspicion elsewhere and call attention to the whole Yarnell Street incident. But if it brought out the other guy, so much the better. No sign of that one all these years. Maybe he's already dead. I can hope.'

'As a matter of fact, we just found out he turned up dead last year.'

'There's a relief. So they're all gone now.'

'Uh huh. Nestor Lowell wasn't an issue anymore, was he, since you'd already taken care of him, way back at the get-go?'

'Damn, you have done your homework.'

'Why, Andy?'

'Oh, hell, that lazy SOB Valenzuela, he wasn't about to do anything. I couldn't believe he caught that case. Didn't matter it was a cop's kid. *My* kid! He might have closed the case if they all walked into the station and bit him on the knee. And that snot-nosed kid who was his partner wasn't worth anything either. Five minutes after talking to them, I knew what I had to do.'

'How could you be sure it was those three? What if it was someone else?'

'I was convinced it had to be them. And it turned out I was right, didn't it?'

Leon hesitated a moment. 'You know Valenzuela's dead, right?'

'No. I didn't know that. Haven't had contact with him since . . . since all that.'

'My point is you don't have to protect him anymore, Andy. I have a pretty good idea why you felt so sure it was those three, and how you knew Nestor's address. I bet you knew all three of the kids' names and addresses. Bobby knew the kids. He was as cynical about Sycamore PD as you, and he was sure they'd blow it, and maybe like you say, he was lazy, too. He figured it was more efficient to give you those addresses.'

Andy was quiet, but Leon could feel it. He was right. Detective Valenzuela had turned Andy into an avenging angel before his son had been dead twenty-four hours. Finally Andy simply said, 'The partner, Truax, knew nothing about it. Nobody else did.'

'So you went after them that morning, figuring to just exterminate them all, bang bang bang. You only got one of them, though.'

'Uh huh. He lived by himself so I figured he'd be the easiest. And he was.'

'And clearly nobody ever found him. Efficient disposal.'

Andy nodded gravely. 'And he never will be found. In fact I did too good a job. The second knucklehead was actually dumb enough to get picked up by two Sycamore uniforms, and then they decided they couldn't hold him. That whole department is like the Keystone Kops in those old silent movies. By the time I had finished, well, cleaning up after his buddy, they'd released him. The moment they let him loose, he bolted. Just evaporated. The third guy, the young kid, was already in the wind.'

'That was Tobias. Surprised you didn't

track him down.'

Andy shook his head. 'I looked, believe me. You know it's not as easy as they make it out to be, to find someone who doesn't want to be found.'

'No, it's not.'

'It's a giant game of hide and seek. That kid just hid in plain sight, a few hundred miles away.'

'So you had to wait until he turned up, which was when he got arrested three years later.'

'I knew it was just a matter of time before he made some noise. Knuckleheads like him always mess up again and again. But then I had to wait until he got out of the joint. I couldn't find any way to reach in.'

'That's a long time to be planning revenge, Andy.'

'I'd have waited until hell froze over. The feeling never softened. You've got kids.'

'You know I do. Two of them.'

'Then you understand what it would be like to have them taken from you.'

'Honestly, I don't. I can't comprehend what that was like, Andy.'

'I pray to God you never do, Leon. When they killed Drew, they killed me. Nobody's got any idea how much died inside of me. But all the worse, it destroyed Kelsey, just cut the heart right out of her. Changed her completely. She never wanted another kid.'

'You stayed together all those years.'

'Thank God for that.' Andy stared off at the rolling surf in the distance. 'Not easy for either of us. Not for a minute.'

'You're taking this all pretty calmly, Andy.'

'It was all inevitable, Leon. I hoped to forestall it, but I've known for years how this had to play out. It's endgame. I told Kelsey all about it today. I'd already made some financial arrangements so she'll be okay. There was nowhere else for this to go.'

'*Okay,*' Leon repeated, shaking his head. He doubted Kelsey would ever be 'okay.' He began to realize how little he really knew his friend Andy Vernon. 'Was it worth it?'

'I'll be asking myself that question for a long time. I honestly don't know. But I have to tell you, I'm more at peace with this than I thought I might be. More than I've been in a long time. I hope my maker feels the same way when the time comes.' He turned to Leon. 'So is this where you call in the troops to bring me in?'

A deep sense of sorrow filled Leon as he pulled out his phone and started to type out a text. 'You better go tell Kelsey goodbye.'

Andy surprisingly did not take very long. Clearly they had already prepared themselves for this. When he returned to the front door, he was alone, and Art, Dan and Jilly were just walking up to the porch. Kelsey had not accompanied him to meet the detectives. Leon could hear a soft sobbing coming from the parlor beyond the screen door. He considered saying goodbye to her and expressing his regret, but thought better of it.

$$\star \quad \star \quad \star$$

'Art told me I'd find you out here.'

Leon looked up from his seat on a low wall in the department parking lot. He had been staring down, unmindful of the police vehicles passing back and forth.

Jilly sat next to him. 'Mind if I join you for a minute?'

'Sure. Just came out here to grab a smoke.'

'You don't smoke anymore, Leon.'

He held his empty hands out sheepishly. 'I guess I just wanted to sit.'

'Are you okay?'

'I'll be fine . . . in a while. This one took a lot out of me. I thought about taking some personal time again after this weekend but decided it'd be better for me to be working.'

The word had come down that Andy Vernon had made a complete statement of confession early that Monday morning. There would be a public announcement for the media forthcoming shortly.

'I'm sorry about Andy. It had to be tough on you.'

'I really didn't want it to be true. I guess I fought it.' Leon shook his head. 'You were right. It was too close to home.'

'Leon, we might not have broken this one without you. You were a critical part of the investigation.'

'I think that's what bothers me the most.'

Jilly, taken aback, waited several beats before answering that. 'Suppose it had come down differently. Suppose Andy had gotten away with it. Could you have lived with knowing that?'

'No. Of course not.'

'Or if the case had gone a different way, maybe if Andy made a run for it . . . or worse? Would that have been any better?'

'No. No, it wouldn't.'

'Everything was going to transpire the way it did, no matter what you did. We speak for the victim. You made a difference in closing it quickly and cleanly.'

'Thanks. But that doesn't change things. Andy was like a second father to me. I didn't want it to be him.'

'I get it.' Jilly thought back on all she had learned from her own former partner and how his death had affected her, how she still missed him. The parking lot seemed weirdly still for a long time. Finally she broke the awkward interlude.

'Dan made some calls this morning. He passed on all the information, including how to contact Sister Cilla, to Sycamore PD.'

'They'll shuffle it to Cold Cases. There's nothing any of them can do about it now.'

'They'll close the case. Someone will care. You can tell Mary Evelyn.'

Leon nodded. 'I plan to do that today.'

'Dan also called Eline Fong and informed her that Xi Lin's statement had led to an arrest and confession, and that there would be no need for her to testify in court as a witness. It seems that Xi Lin had a long conversation with her aunt over the weekend and declared she wanted to return home to China. The conversation actually shook her. Apparently Ms. Fong is not such a monster, but she's very set in her ways. She came to an agreement with her niece to give her more free time to learn English and become more socialized here, maybe get her started in school, if she agreed to stay. In fact she asked Dan if he'd be willing to help them.'

'That could be interesting. What'd he say to that?'

'I think he might take them up on it.

Dan's parents are first generation here. He understands the difficulties.'

'Looks like some people will come out of this all right, anyway. That's all to the good.'

'What about Kelsey? What's she going to do?'

'I don't know. I don't have it in me to talk to her yet. It might be a while. I've got no idea how she feels about me right now.' Leon shook his head. 'She probably blames me for taking down Andy. I can't fault her if she does.'

'Andy doesn't seem to hold it against you. Neither of them should. It was Andy who tracked the vics down and killed them in cold blood. And premeditated or not, it led to his killing a third man.'

Leon stared directly into Jilly's eyes. 'If it had been me, I can't say that I wouldn't have done exactly the same thing. I can't imagine if that had been one of my kids.'

'Having no kids of my own, I certainly can't imagine either. Maybe I could have done it too. But no matter how understandable, it would still have been wrong. Someone would have come after you or me. And they would have been right.' She laid a hand on his shoulder and felt the tension in his muscles. 'You're a good detective, Leon, and a good man. One of the best. You did the right thing.'

'I know that. I also know that doing the right thing doesn't always make you feel all that great.'

'Leon, are you a religious man?'

'I suppose. I mean, I go to church. What about you?'

'No, not really.'

'And the reason you ask this is . . . ?'

'I'm just thinking. Two men with violent pasts died looking for something. Redemption. Forgiveness. Whatever you want to call it, I suppose it comes down to a search for inner peace, for absolution from the consequences of their actions. I wonder if either of them ever found it.'

'Andy was looking for peace too.'

'I know, by a very different route.'

'If you're asking me if I think that was the right route, I don't know what to tell you.'

Before Jilly could answer, the strains of Haydn started up from her phone, but it sounded odd. Then she realized it was being overlaid what sounded like a saxophone — from Leon's phone. They both picked up and moments later almost simultaneously uttered, 'I'll be right in.'

They stood up, pocketing their phones, laughing despite themselves at the synchronized movements. Leon smiled wryly.

'So much for post-mortems. Par for the course around here, huh? Duty calls.'

As they hurried towards the front door, Jilly reflected that maybe that the constant distraction of their chosen walk of life was all for the best.

We do hope that you have enjoyed reading this large print book.

Did you know that all of our titles are available for purchase?

We publish a wide range of high quality large print books including:
Romances, Mysteries, Classics
General Fiction
Non Fiction and Westerns

Special interest titles available in large print are:
The Little Oxford Dictionary
Music Book, Song Book
Hymn Book, Service Book

Also available from us courtesy of Oxford University Press:
Young Readers' Dictionary
(large print edition)
Young Readers' Thesaurus
(large print edition)

For further information or a free brochure, please contact us at:
Ulverscroft Large Print Books Ltd.,
The Green, Bradgate Road, Anstey,
Leicester, LE7 7FU, England.
Tel: (00 44) **0116 236 4325**
Fax: (00 44) **0116 234 0205**

Other titles in the
Linford Mystery Library:

MURDER GETS AROUND

Robert Sidney Bowen

Murder and mayhem begin innocently enough at the Rankins' cocktail party, where Gerry Barnes and his fiery red-haired girlfriend Paula Grant while away a few carefree hours. There, Gerry meets René DeFoe, who wishes to engage his services as a private investigator, for undisclosed reasons — an assignment Gerry reluctantly accepts. But the next morning, when Gerry enters his office to keep his appointment, he finds René murdered on the premises. He puts his own life at risk as he investigates why a corpse was made of his client . . .

THE LAST STEP

The victim, found shot to death on a public stairway, is a recently paroled prison inmate. Is it a deliberate act of vengeance, and does it mean the killer will be looking for more victims? Detectives Jilly Garvey and Dan Lee are put on the case; but their colleague Leon Simpkins, who has taken an unexpected interest, seems to find it all striking uncomfortably close to home. Before they can solve the crime, the three will have to uncover deep secrets, with a profound effect on almost everyone involved.

Books by Tony Gleeson
in the Linford Mystery Library:

NIGHT MUSIC
IT'S HER FAULT
A QUESTION OF GUILT
THE OTHER FRANK
JESSICA'S DEATH
SOMETIMES THEY DIE
THE PIEMAN'S LAST SONG